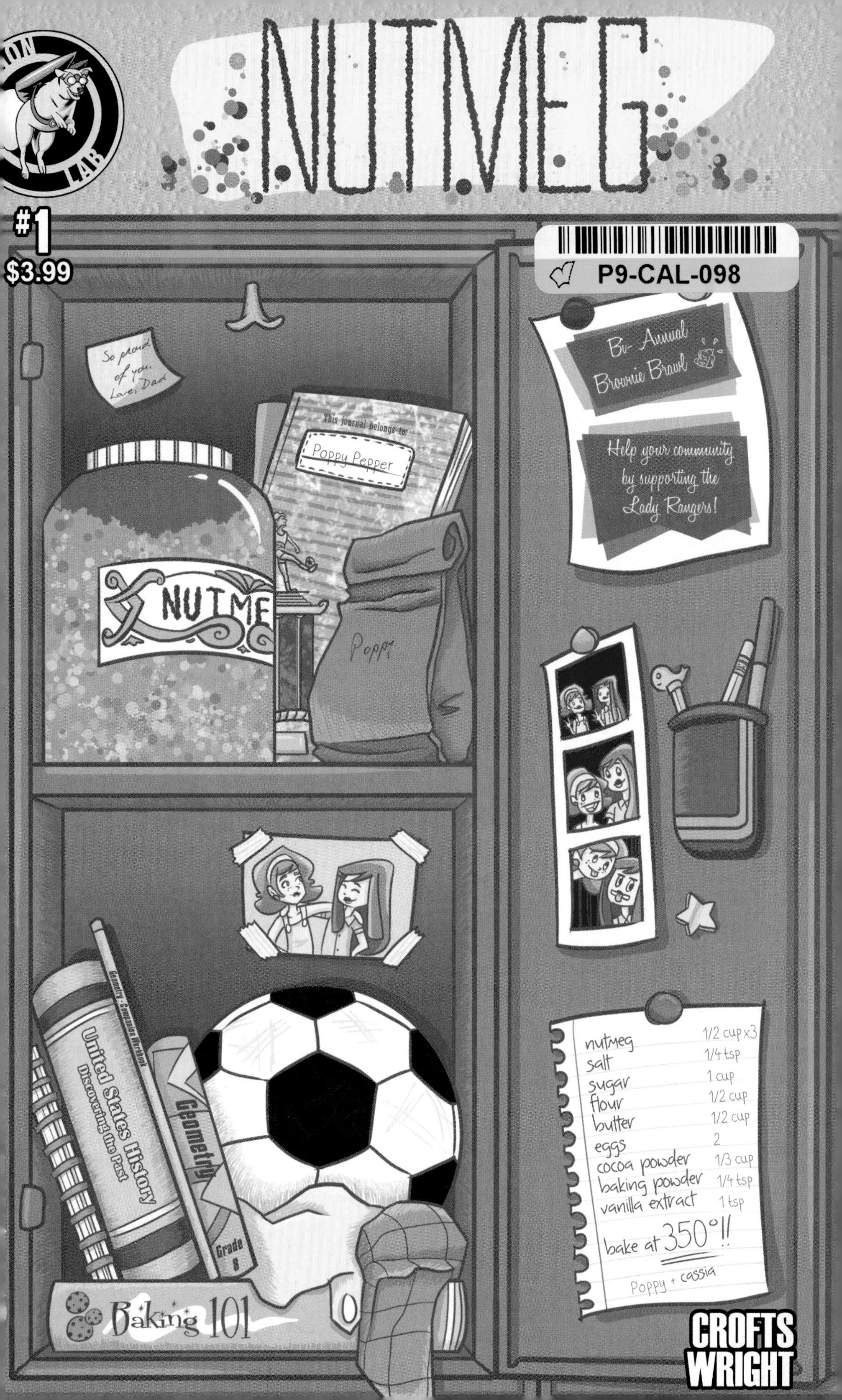

NUTMEG
#1
$3.99
P9-CAL-098
So proud of you. Love, Dad
This journal belongs to:
Poppy Pepper
NUTME
Poppy
Bi-Annual Brownie Brawl
Help your community by supporting the Lady Rangers!
nutmeg 1/2 cup x3
salt 1/4 tsp
sugar 1 cup
flour 1/2 cup
butter 1/2 cup
eggs 2
cocoa powder 1/3 cup
baking powder 1/4 tsp
vanilla extract 1 tsp
bake at 350°!!
Poppy + cassia
Geometry · Companion Workbook
United States History
Discovering the Past
Geometry
Grade 8
Baking 101
CROFTS
WRIGHT

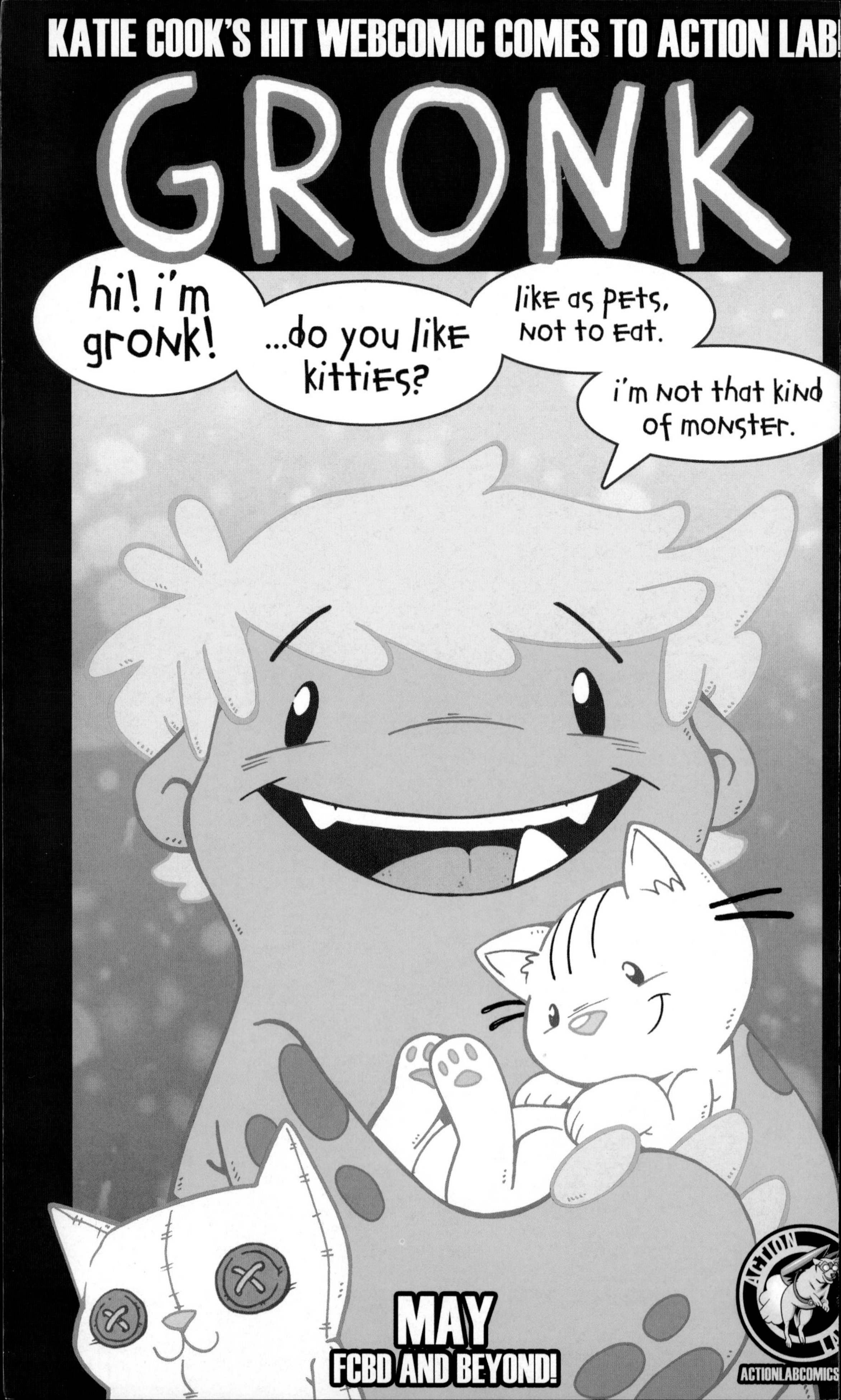
KATIE COOK'S HIT WEBCOMIC COMES TO ACTION LAB!
GRONK
hi! i'm gronk!
...do you like kitties?
like as pets, not to eat.
i'm not that kind of monster.
MAY
FCBD AND BEYOND!
ACTIONLABCOMICS

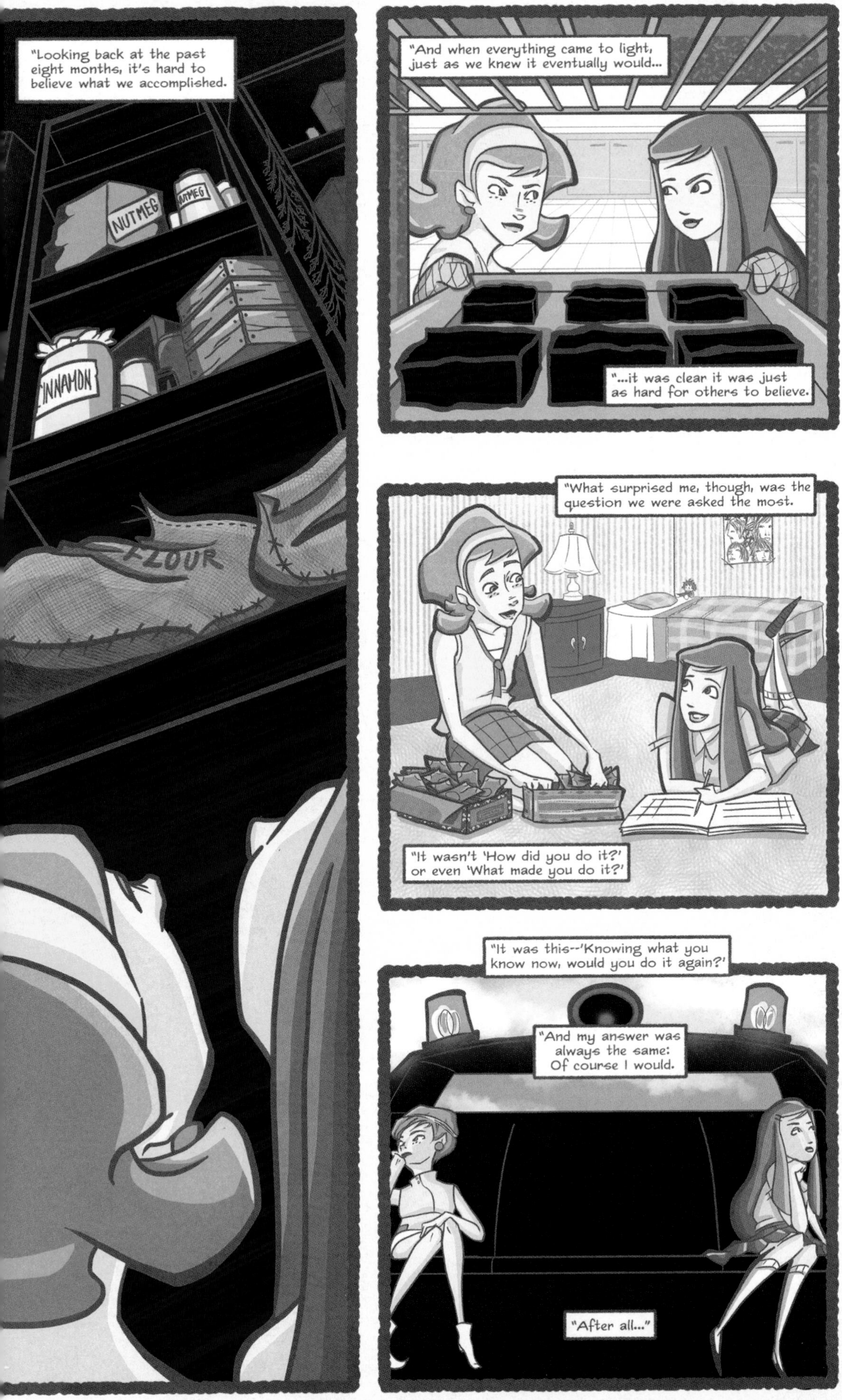
"Looking back at the past eight months, it's hard to believe what we accomplished.
NUTMEG
NUTMEG
CINNAMON
FLOUR
"And when everything came to light, just as we knew it eventually would...
"...it was clear it was just as hard for others to believe.
"What surprised me, though, was the question we were asked the most.
"It wasn't 'How did you do it?' or even 'What made you do it?'
"It was this--'Knowing what you know now, would you do it again?'
"And my answer was always the same: Of course I would.
"After all..."

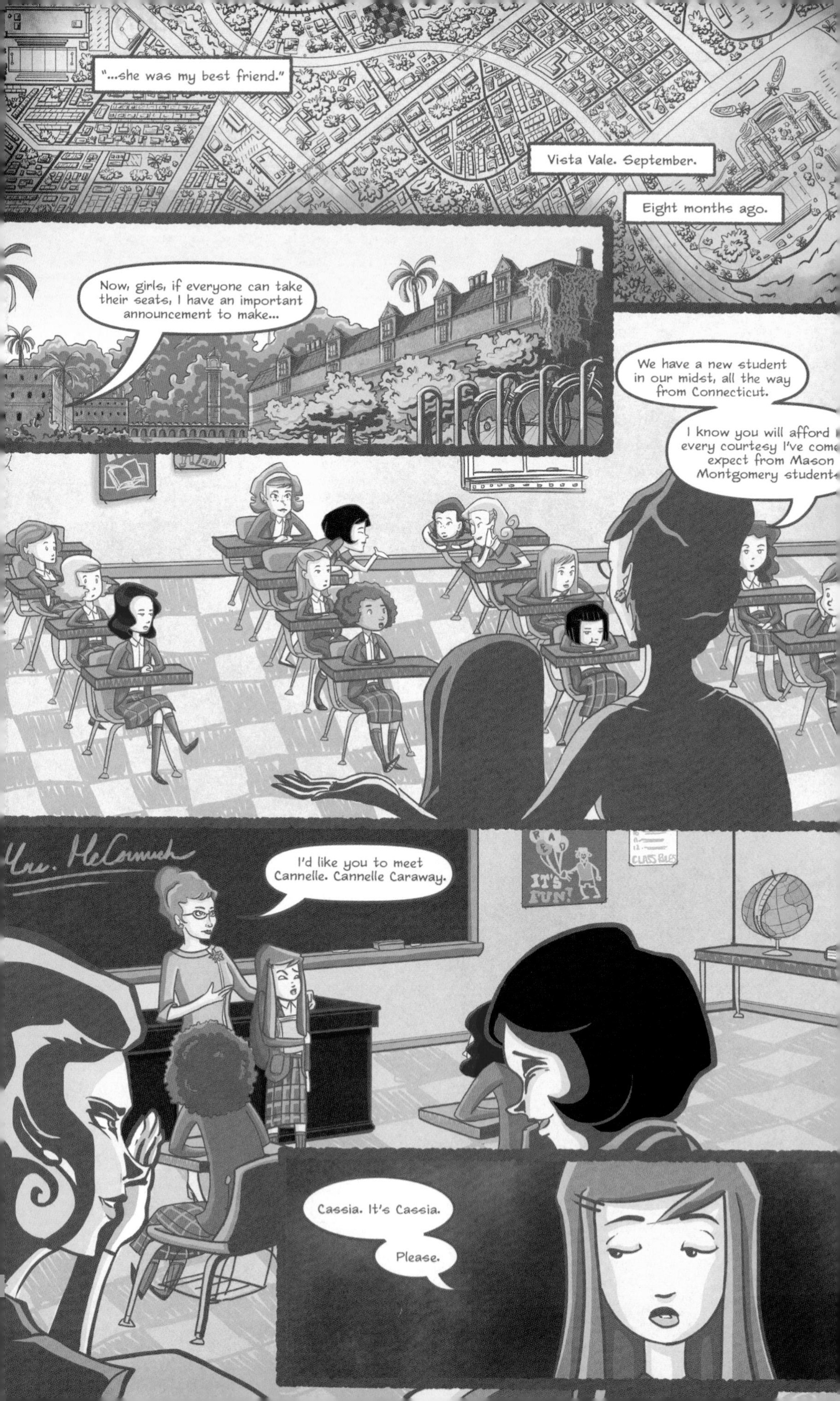
"...she was my best friend."
Vista Vale. September.
Eight months ago.
Now, girls, if everyone can take their seats, I have an important announcement to make...
We have a new student in our midst, all the way from Connecticut.
I know you will afford every courtesy I've come expect from Mason Montgomery students.
I'd like you to meet Cannelle. Cannelle Caraway.
IT'S FUN!
CLASS RULES
Cassia. It's Cassia.
Please.

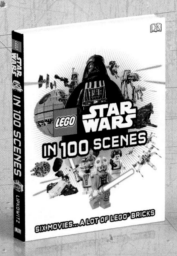

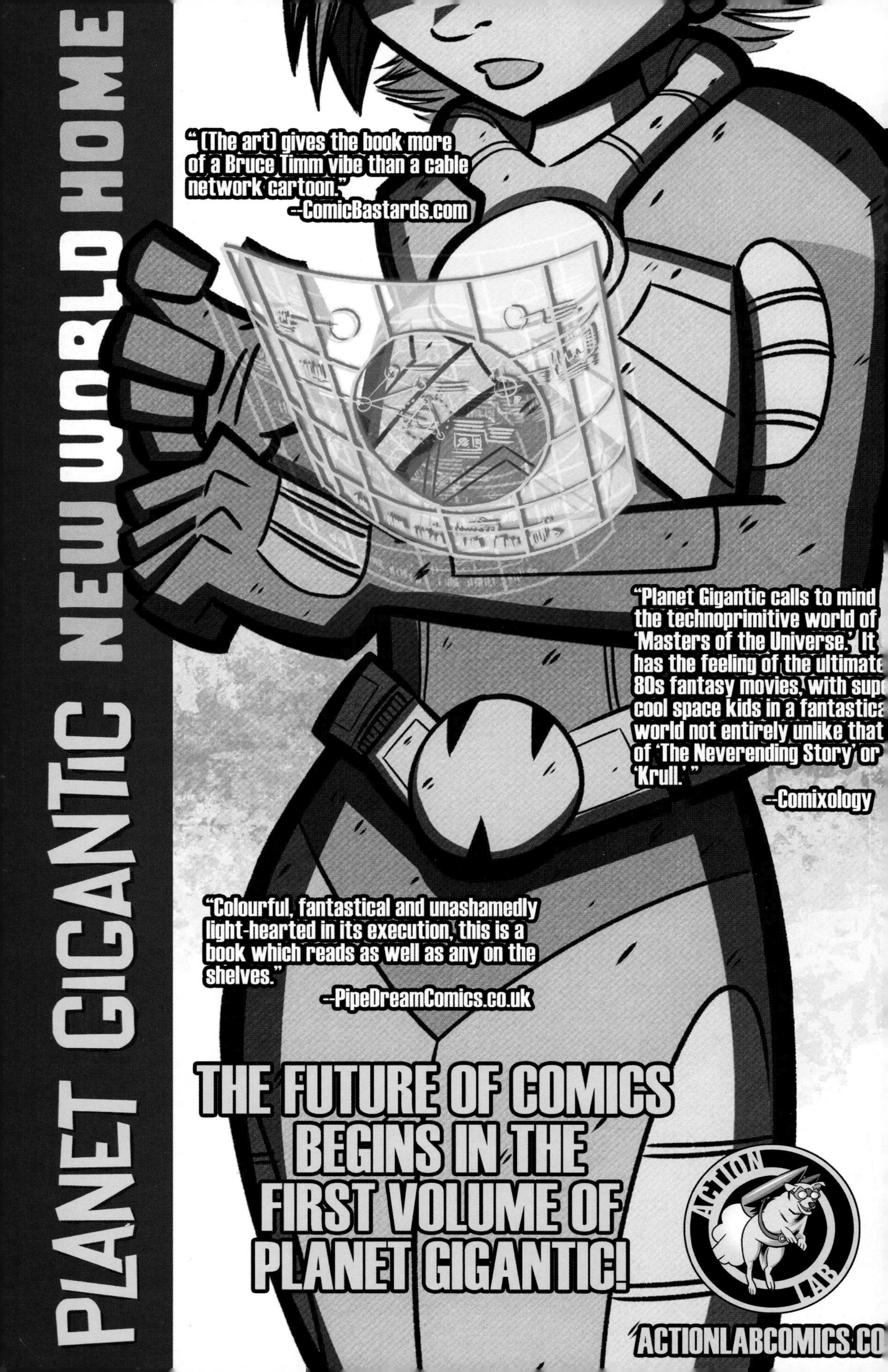
PLANET GIGANTIC NEW WORLD HOME
" (The art) gives the book more of a Bruce Timm vibe than a cable network cartoon."
--ComicBastards.com
"Planet Gigantic calls to mind the technoprimitive world of 'Masters of the Universe.' It has the feeling of the ultimate 80s fantasy movies, with supe cool space kids in a fantastica world not entirely unlike that of 'The Neverending Story' or 'Krull.' "
--Comixology
"Colourful, fantastical and unashamedly light-hearted in its execution, this is a book which reads as well as any on the shelves."
--PipeDreamComics.co.uk
THE FUTURE OF COMICS BEGINS IN THE FIRST VOLUME OF PLANET GIGANTIC!
ACTION LAB
ACTIONLABCOMICS.CO

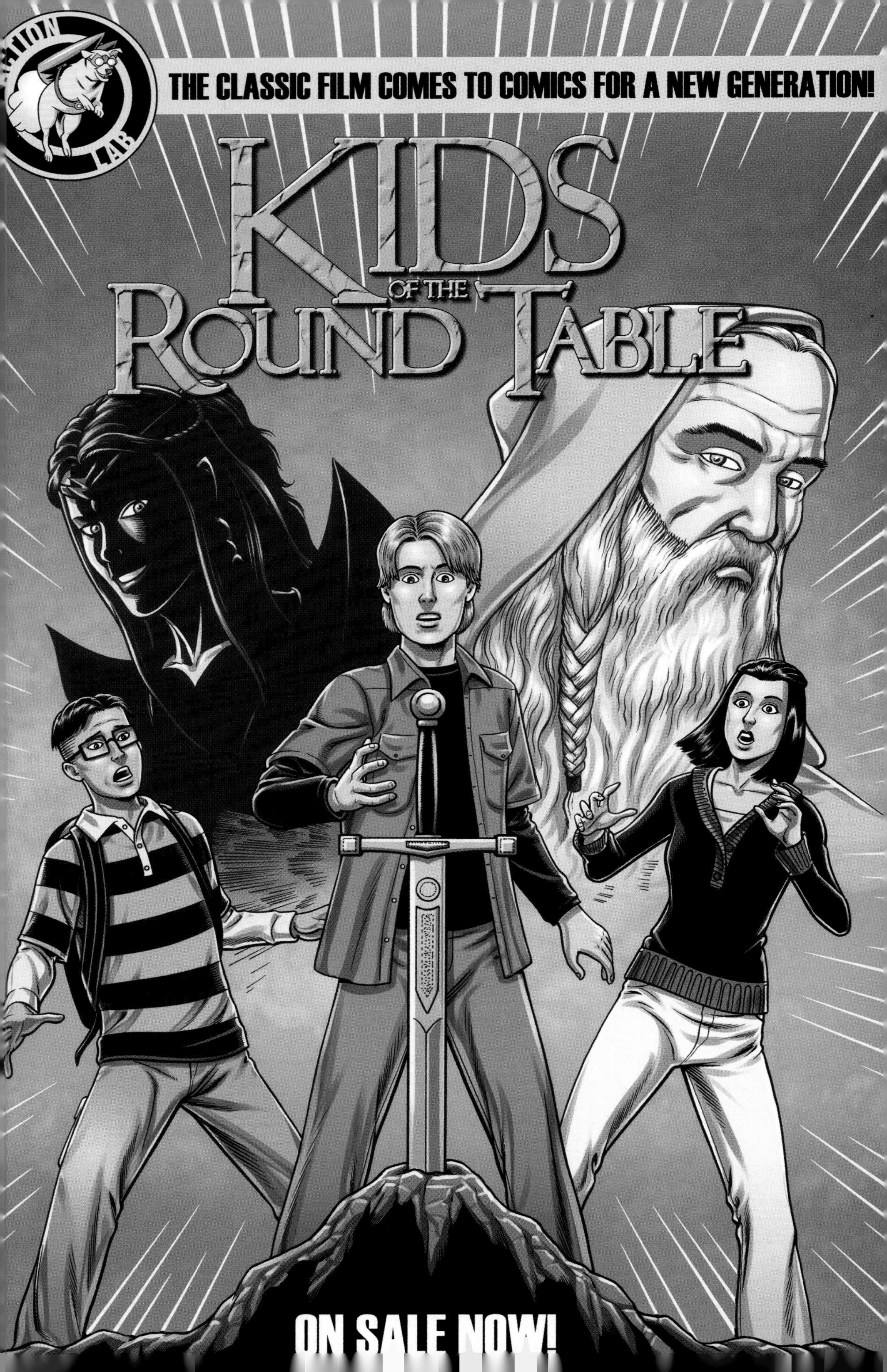
ACTION LAB
THE CLASSIC FILM COMES TO COMICS FOR A NEW GENERATION!
KIDS OF THE ROUND TABLE
ON SALE NOW!

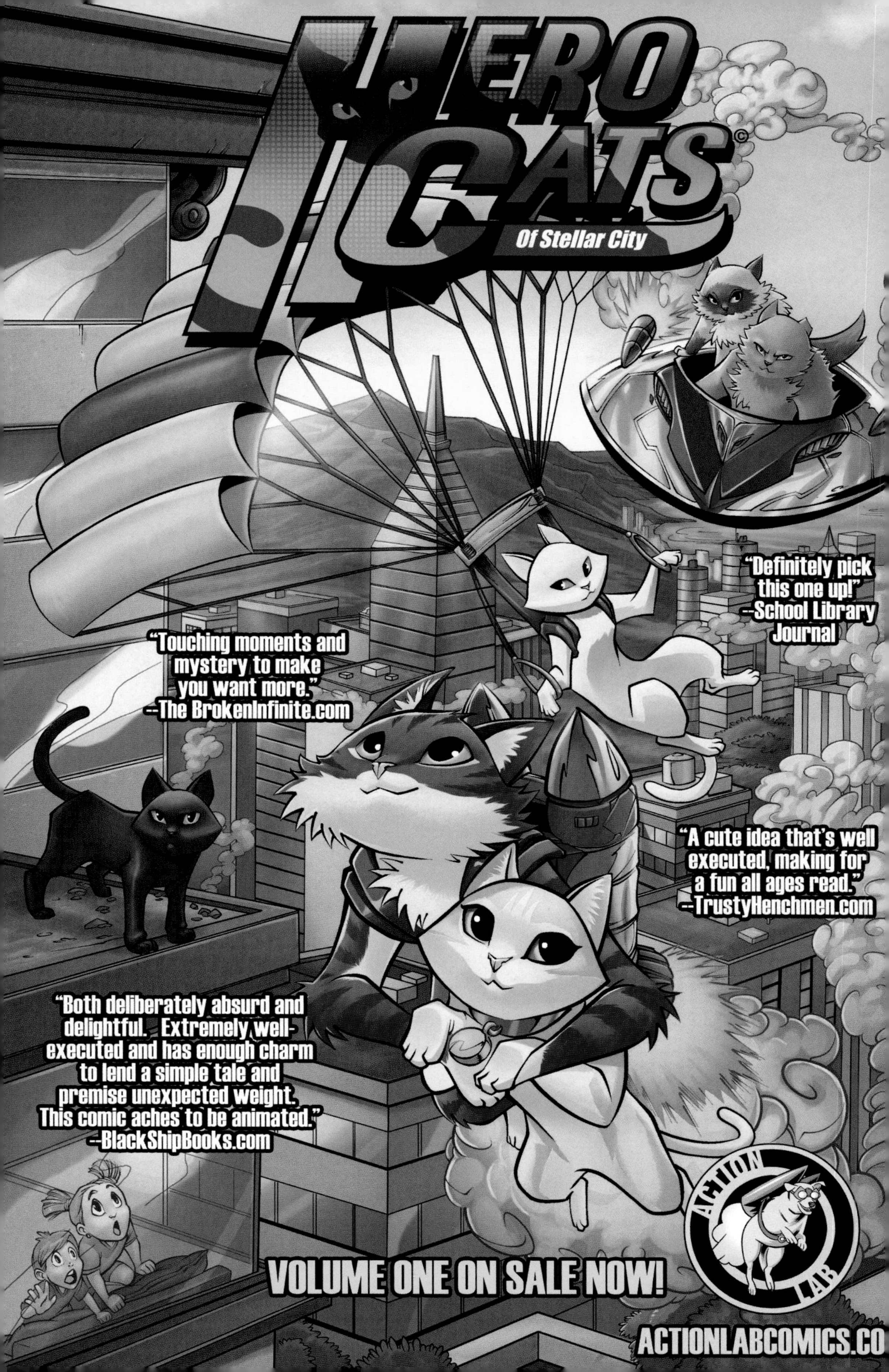
HERO CATS
Of Stellar City
"Definitely pick this one up!" --School Library Journal
"Touching moments and mystery to make you want more." --The BrokenInfinite.com
"A cute idea that's well executed, making for a fun all ages read." --TrustyHenchmen.com
"Both deliberately absurd and delightful. Extremely well-executed and has enough charm to lend a simple tale and premise unexpected weight. This comic aches to be animated." --BlackShipBooks.com
ACTION LAB
VOLUME ONE ON SALE NOW!
ACTIONLABCOMICS.CO

THE PIRATE PRINCESS

AVAILABLE IN FINER STORES EVERYWHERE

The complete collected edition of Princeless: The Pirate Princess. Adrienne has been on the run and working to save her sisters, but when she finds another princess locked away in a tower, she decides to spring her! But Raven Xingtao, the daughter of the Pirate King, is more of a handful that Adrienne could have ever expected. Before she knows it, Adrienne is off on a whirlwind adventure to complete Raven's quest for revenge!

INGREDIENTS

---

1 Cup of all-purpose flour (sifted)
¾ tsp of baking soda
½ tsp of salt (optional)
1 Tbsp of cinnamon
¼ tsp of nutmeg
¾ Cup of butter (softened)
1 1/3 Cup of firmly packed brown sugar
2 eggs
1 tsp of vanilla
3 Cups of oats (uncooked)
½ to 1 Cup of chocolate chips (or raisins)

DIRECTIONS

---

1. Preheat oven to 350°F (180°C)

2. Sift together the flour, baking soda, salt, cinnamon and nutmeg in Bowl #1.

3. In Bowl #2, mix butter and sugar until smooth.

4. Add the eggs and vanilla to Bowl #2 and beat for two minutes until smooth.

5. Mix Bowl #1 and Bowl #2 together.

6. Stir in oats and chocolate chips (or raisins).

7. Grease a baking sheet.

8. Drop spoonfuls of the cookie batter on the pan.

9. Bake for 10-12 minutes.

10. Let cookies cool and then dig in!

YUKA'S OATMEAL COOKIES
(WITH OPTIONAL CHOCOLATE CHIPS OR RAISINS)

Hi all, James here!

(You know, we should come up with a name for Nutmeg readers, so if you have any ideas, let us know!)

This month's recipe comes from Yuka, one of my favorite people in the whole world and who actually probably saved my life. I mean that in the least dramatic, hyperbolic way possible, of course.

I met Yuka in the summer of 2004, when she and I and a bunch of other cool and lucky people, were selected to participate in the Japan Exchange & Teaching (or, JET) Programme. As Assistant Language Teachers (or, ALTs) on this program, we would be working in conjunction with Japanese teachers of English to help expand the linguistic and cultural understanding of Japanese junior and senior high school students. At the time, I was a full year removed from college graduation (Hail Pitt!), but somehow in my four years at university I'd learned to cook maybe three things. (Thank goodness my neighbors, Desiree and Justice, made plenty of food and were happy to share with us.)

The point being, as a new arrival in Japan, particularly one in the distant, rural seaside town of Tottori, I was going to have to learn to fend for myself very quickly. And part of that meant learning to cook.

At first I would just try to experiment with simple stuff, but it wasn't long before Yuka began giving me pointers and suggestions. Then, when she saw that I was really trying to make a go of this cooking thing, she got me a cookbook—The Working Parents Cookbook by Jeff and Jodie Morgan, to be precise. Basically, it was a cookbook with easy-to-follow recipes of a wide variety that also didn't take too long to prepare. Thus armed, I'd set up challenges for myself a few days a week to try out different recipes in the book. (The other challenge was finding the Japanese names for the ingredients in what I was looking to make.) And I was making—or attempting to make—everything from adobo to mayonnaise to stir fry and back again.

As I grew my repertoire thanks to this book and Yuka's tips, I was able to cut back more on dining out, which helped preserve my income and waistline. She didn't just introduce me to a life skill, she helped me see how fun it could be, and I think that was instrumental in keeping me grounded through the ups and downs of teaching in a foreign country.

So, thank you for that, Yuka! And thanks for letting us print your Oatmeal Cookie recipe!

- James

While *Nutmeg* doesn't involve a love story at the center stage, it's really about the way the characters interract with each other that makes it fun to read. I'm always excited to get the next script and find out what happens. When you have a huge cast of characters like the ones that Mason Montgomery Prep contains, I think the most exciting part is seeing what these characters who we thought we knew so well will do next. It may not always be what we're expecting, because people are unpredictable and have depth, and James does an amazing job at capturing that.

Cassia essentially faces the same situation that Sandy did. She's dropped into a place she doesn't know and immediately has to hold her own. Of course, she befriends Poppy but how well do these two girls actually know each other outside of their common goal of taking down Saffron? On the other side, how well do we really know Saffron and Marjorie? No one is straight good or bad, they're just people who make decisions that are sometimes good or bad and those decisions are influenced by so many external and internal factors.

I could talk all day about how there are parallels within the story aspects between the two, but let's talk a little bit about the aesthetic part. The colors were are such an expressive and important part of the book and I found inspiration in many places. From the soft vintage look of Wes Anderson movies, to graphic novles such as Daniel Clowes' *Ghost World* and the style of any Chris Ware book, I have wanted to make something as stand out as much as these creators that I look up to. *Grease* influenced me with it's pastel colors and costumes that give an undertone of innocence and wholesomeness that makes everything seem so unasuming. I wanted to give that look to the book because behind all the sweetness that Poppy and Cassia display, there's a sharp bite to their personalities. The same goes for the other characters and the situations they deal with. This is why I'm so grateful that even though we're so far away from each other, the collaborative aspects of working on *Nutmeg* have been a joy.

To match the fantastic writing that James has done, I wanted to be able to capture all of the complexities of the characters through the visuals. I've had a lot of people comment on the softness of the colors and the line work being done in brown instead of the traditional black. Don't worry, it's all been good feedback, and I'm so grateful that you're enjoying it! It was a huge decision from the beginning to go with the soft style, especially with the line work. Once you do something that noticeable, there's no going back from it, but it's worked out well so far.

If you've taken anything away from this installment of The Cooling Rack, I hope it's a *Grease* song that's now stuck in your head. It's because of wonderful people like you that things like *Nutmeg* can exist, and I hope that somewhere out there some day we can be an inspiration for someone else!

Until next time,

Jackie

THE COOLING RACK

CONTACT: @NUTMEGCOMIC · NUTMEGCOMICS@GMAIL.COM

Grease

by Jackie Crofts

First off, if you're reading this that must mean that you just read the third issue of Nutmeg and I want to say THANK YOU! I hide behind James' fancy talkin' words and draw my pictures most of the time, so The Cooling Rack is an awesome thing for me to be able to reach out to you all. Now allow me to spin you a tale of my young hoodlum days.

Some things from your childhood you grow out of, and then there's *Grease*. I had a lot of trouble deciding which influence of mine to talk to you about. While it may not be my favorite among my influences (It's kind of hard to compete with *Twin Peaks*), or something that I watch often anymore, I chose *Grease* because it's something I grew up with. For one reason or another, I had a '50's obsession phase in elementary school and I think parts of that have always stuck with me and in return have really influenced the style and look of *Nutmeg*. I can still remember having '50's parties with my best friends. We'd wear poodle skirts and come up with choreographed dance routines to the songs from *Grease* that we would make our parents watch. We thought we were just about the coolest thing ever.

For our readers who have never seen the movie, it stars Olivia Newton John and John Travolta. They play two star-crossed high school lovers that meet when Olivia Newton John's character, Sandy, has come from Australia to stay in America for her summer vacation. She meets Danny, played by John Travolta, and they spend their summer together but believe they have to part ways when it's time for her to return home. When the new school year starts at Rydell High, they soon discover that Sandy has not only stayed in the states, she's attending the same high school. It follows the ragtag cliques of students within Rydell as they try to deal with social pressures, personal issues, and relationship problems over their senior year. Also, if you haven't picked up on it yet, it is indeed a musical.

One of the core themes of the movie is all about trying to find a sense of belonging, and I think that's why it relates to *Nutmeg* so well. Sandy is not only living in a country that she's unfamiliar with, she's going to a school full of people she doesn't know at all. The girls she thinks she's made friends with can be two-faced and cruel behind her back. Even the other characters who are surrounded by their friends deal with the pressures of trying to fit in around different groups of people, even if it means hurting the ones they care about just to have a certain image. Keeping up appearances in a social landscape that has a pre-established culture is one of the biggest turmoils for anyone, no matter what the age. It's why having a friend you can confide in is such an important thing.

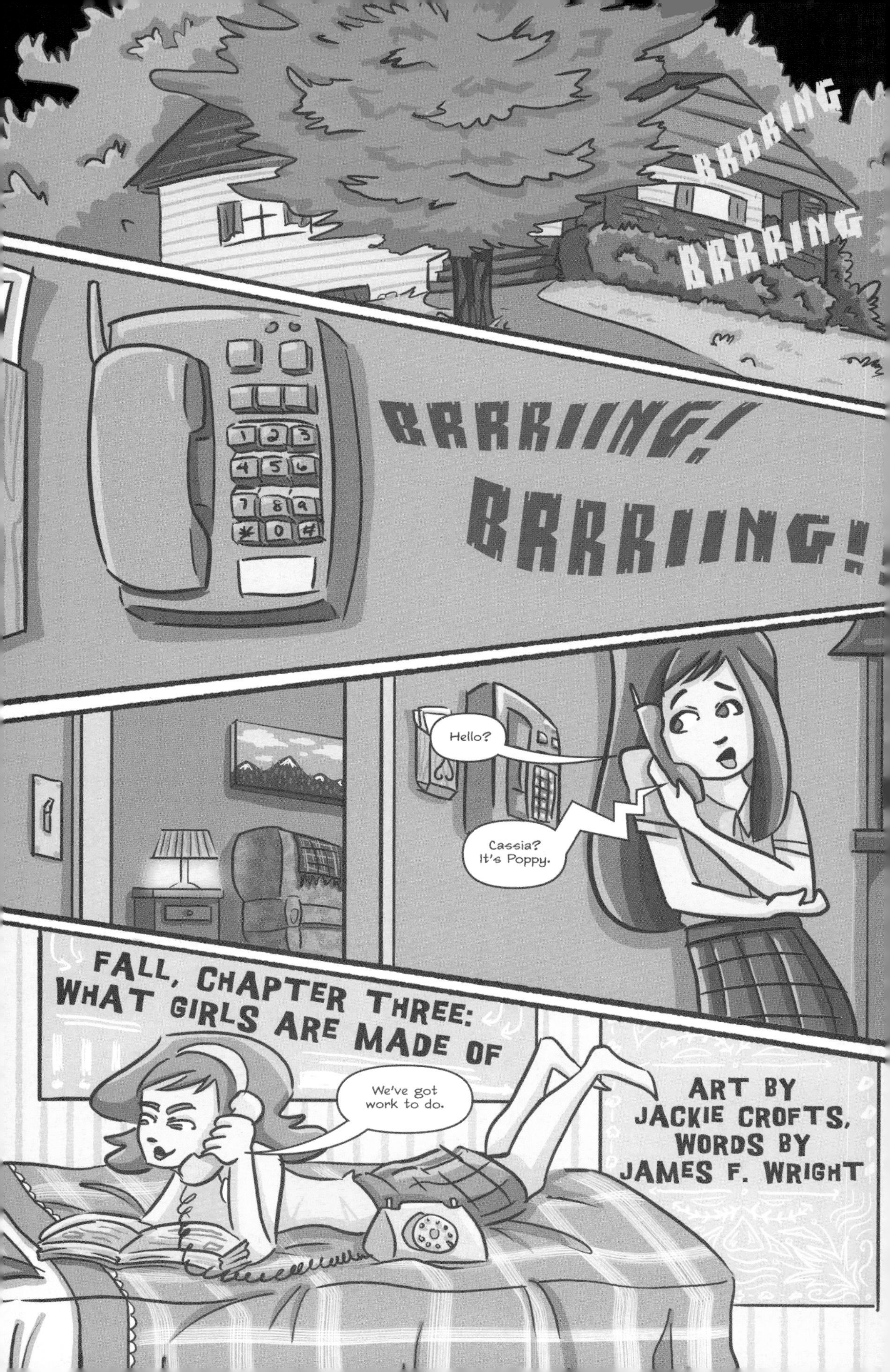
BRRRING
BRRRING
BRRRIING!
BRRRIING!
Hello?
Cassia? It's Poppy.
FALL, CHAPTER THREE: WHAT GIRLS ARE MADE OF
We've got work to do.
ART BY JACKIE CROFTS, WORDS BY JAMES F. WRIGHT

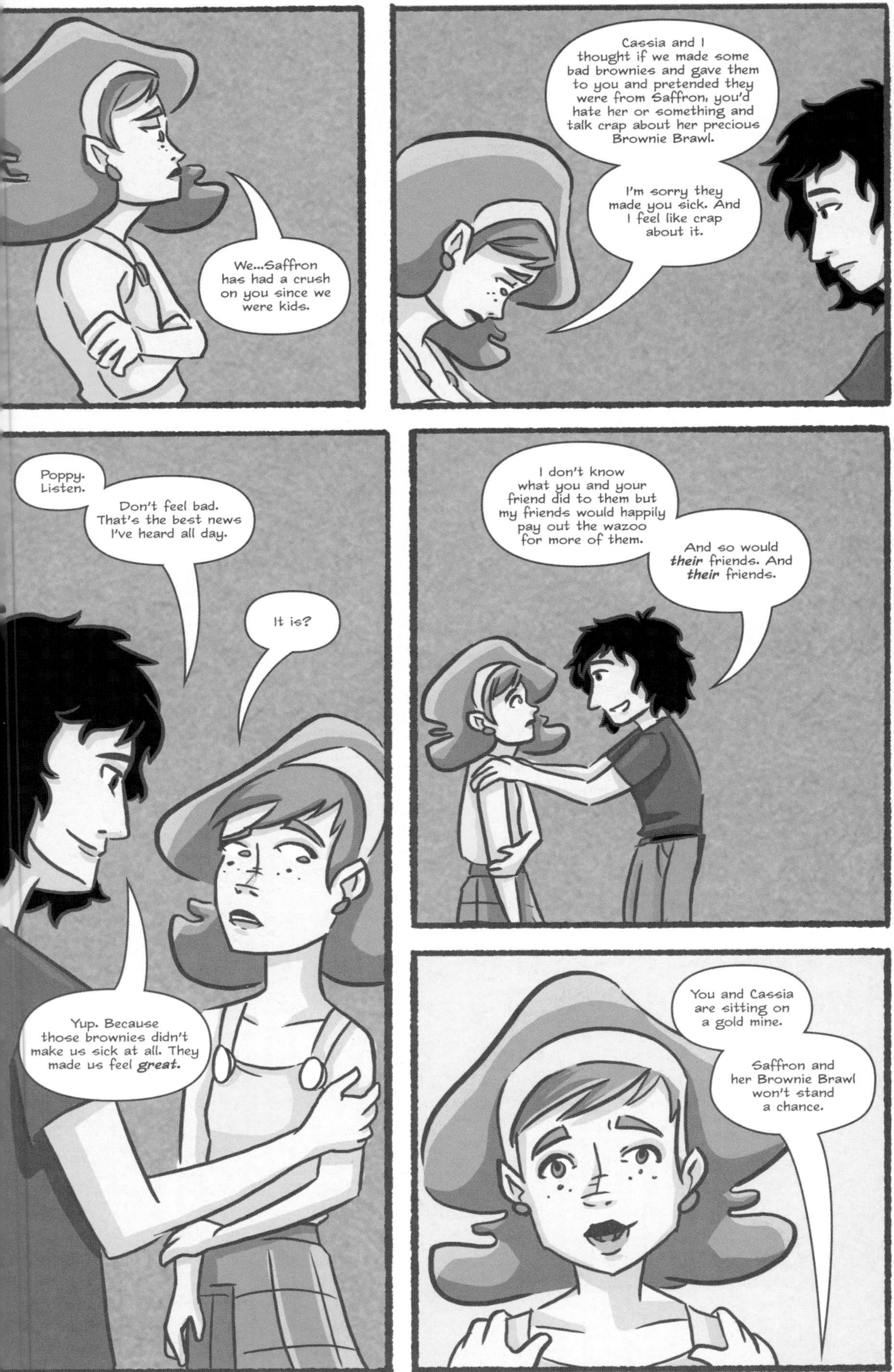
We...Saffron has had a crush on you since we were kids.
Cassia and I thought if we made some bad brownies and gave them to you and pretended they were from Saffron, you'd hate her or something and talk crap about her precious Brownie Brawl.
I'm sorry they made you sick. And I feel like crap about it.
Poppy. Listen.
Don't feel bad. That's the best news I've heard all day.
It is?
Yup. Because those brownies didn't make us sick at all. They made us feel *great*.
I don't know what you and your friend did to them but my friends would happily pay out the wazoo for more of them.
And so would *their* friends. And *their* friends.
You and Cassia are sitting on a gold mine.
Saffron and her Brownie Brawl won't stand a chance.

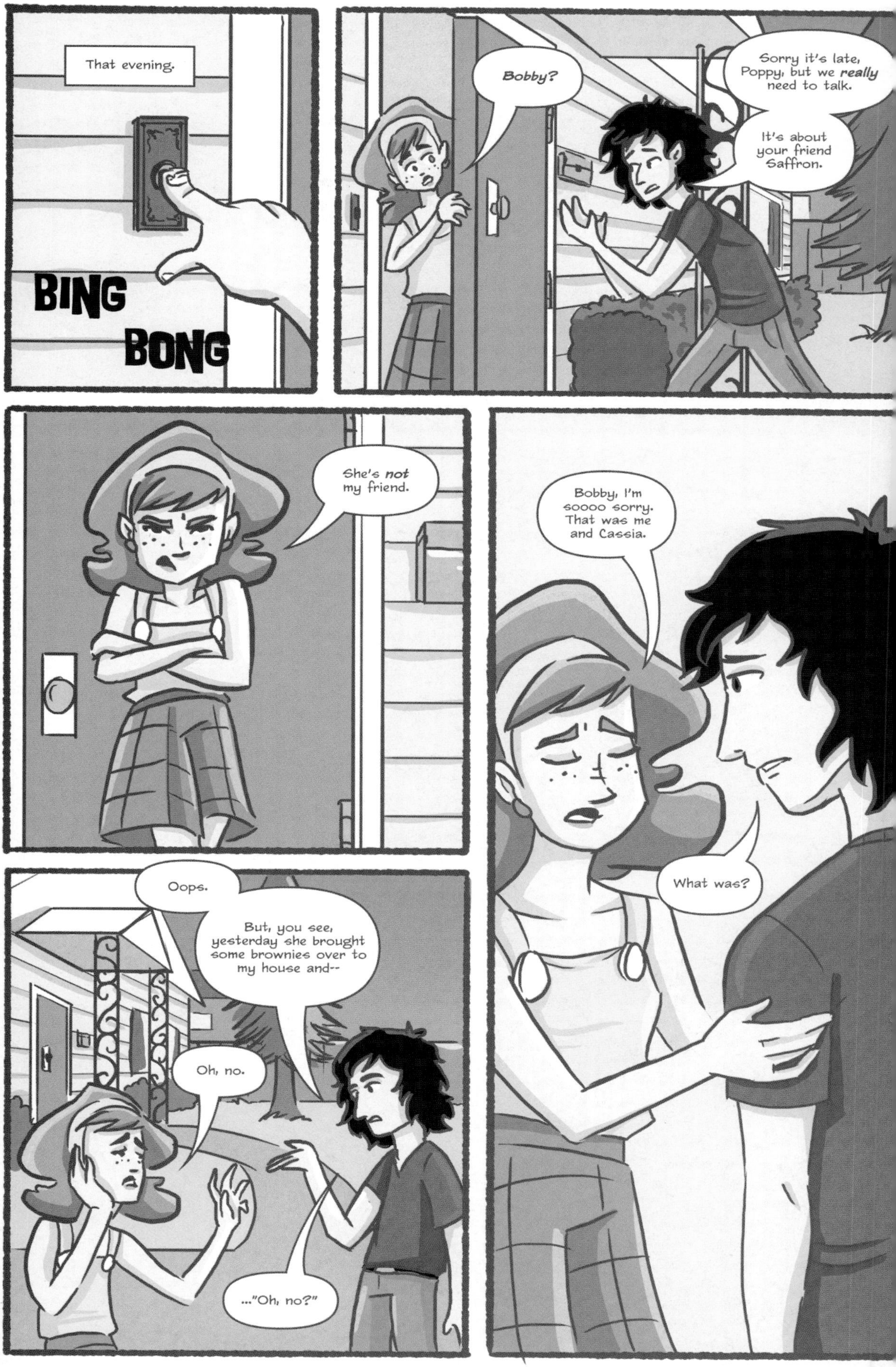
That evening.
BING
BONG
Bobby?
Sorry it's late, Poppy, but we really need to talk.
It's about your friend Saffron.
She's not my friend.
Bobby, I'm soooo sorry. That was me and Cassia.
What was?
Oops.
But, you see, yesterday she brought some brownies over to my house and--
Oh, no.
..."Oh, no?"

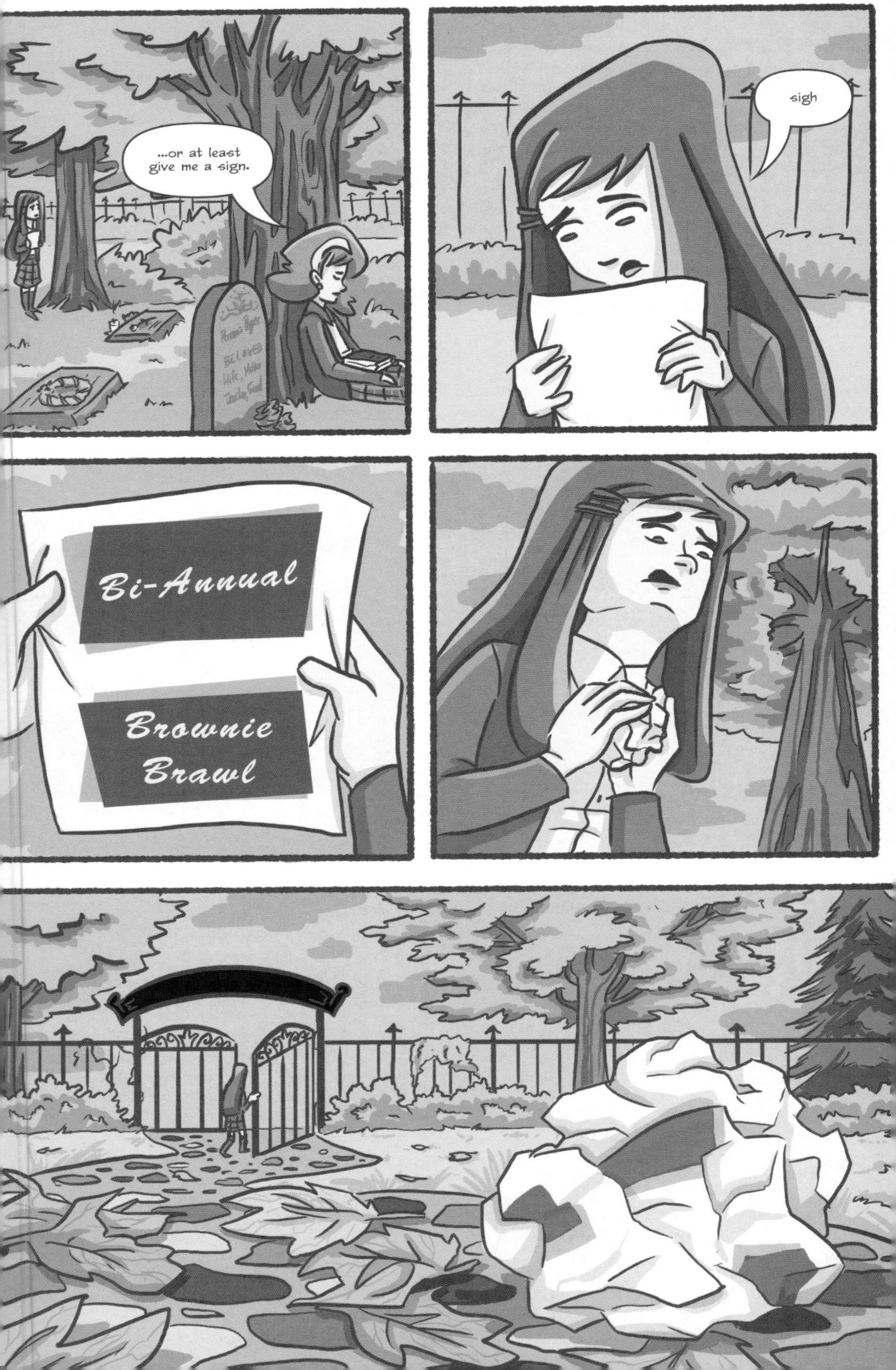
...or at least give me a sign.
sigh
Bi-Annual
Brownie Brawl

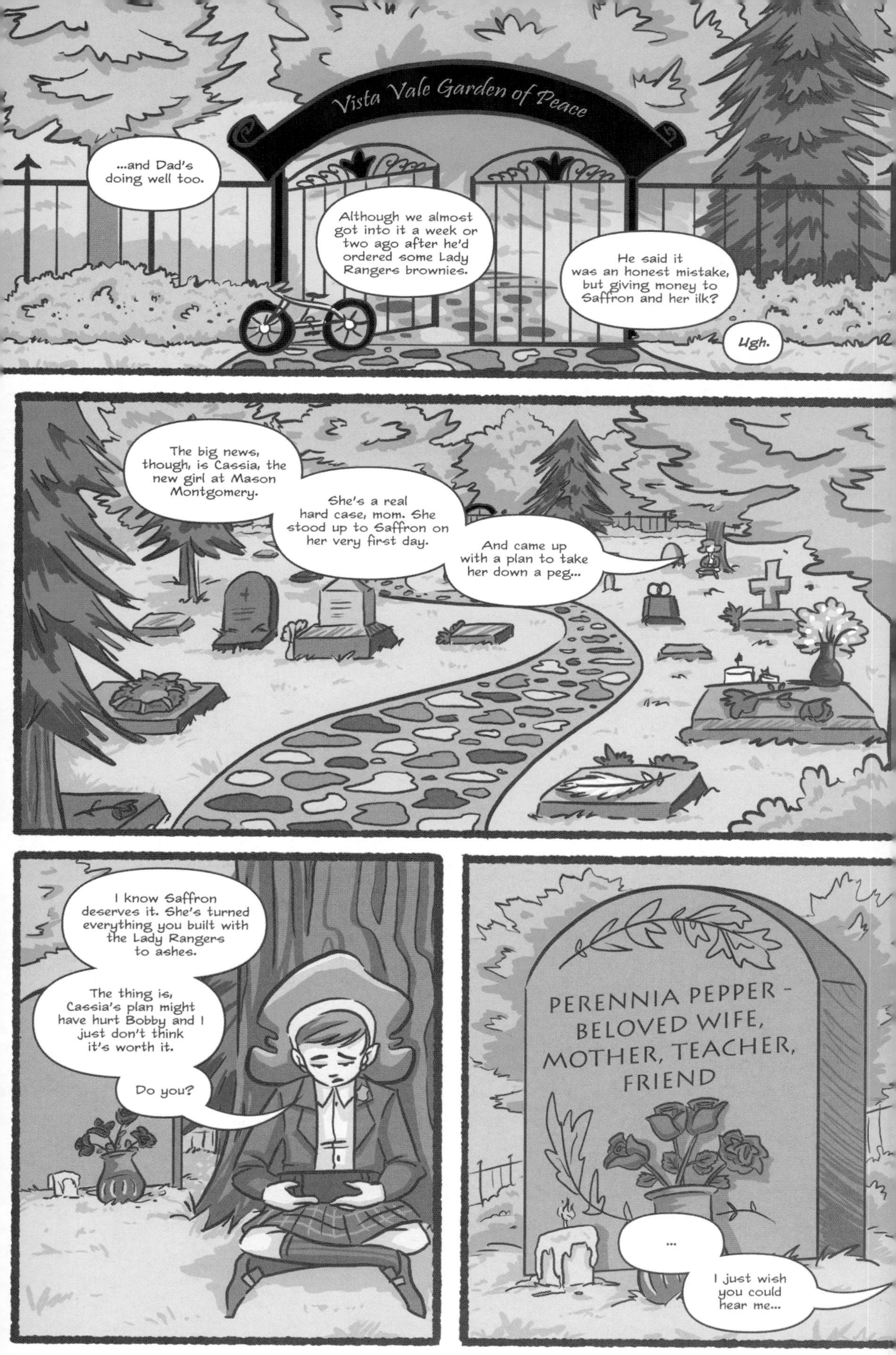
Vista Vale Garden of Peace
...and Dad's doing well too.
Although we almost got into it a week or two ago after he'd ordered some Lady Rangers brownies.
He said it was an honest mistake, but giving money to Saffron and her ilk?
Ugh.
The big news, though, is Cassia, the new girl at Mason Montgomery.
She's a real hard case, mom. She stood up to Saffron on her very first day.
And came up with a plan to take her down a peg...
I know Saffron deserves it. She's turned everything you built with the Lady Rangers to ashes.
The thing is, Cassia's plan might have hurt Bobby and I just don't think it's worth it.
Do you?
PERENNIA PEPPER - BELOVED WIFE, MOTHER, TEACHER, FRIEND
...
I just wish you could hear me...

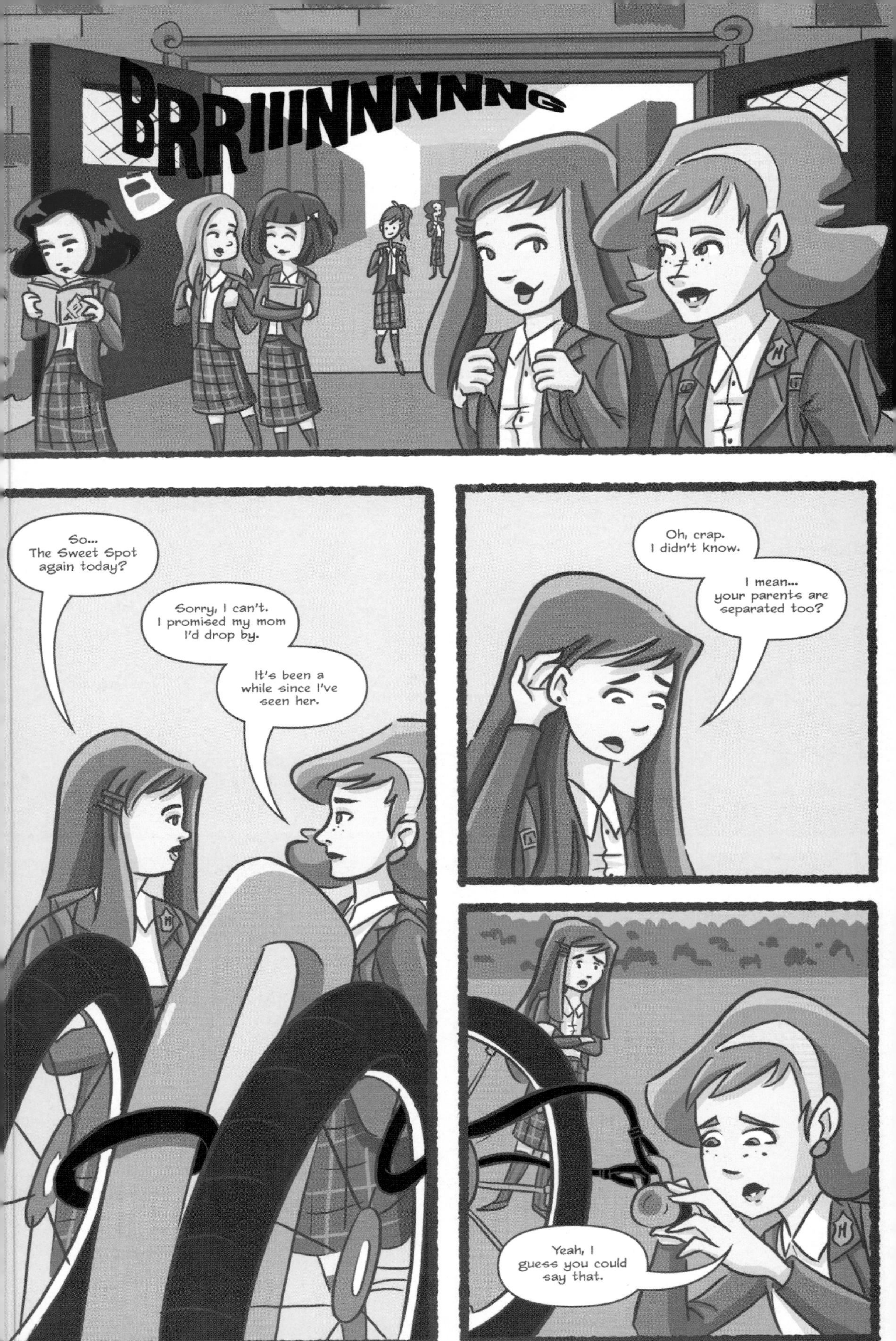
BRRIIINNNNNNG
So... The Sweet Spot again today?
Sorry, I can't. I promised my mom I'd drop by.
It's been a while since I've seen her.
Oh, crap. I didn't know.
I mean... your parents are separated too?
Yeah, I guess you could say that.

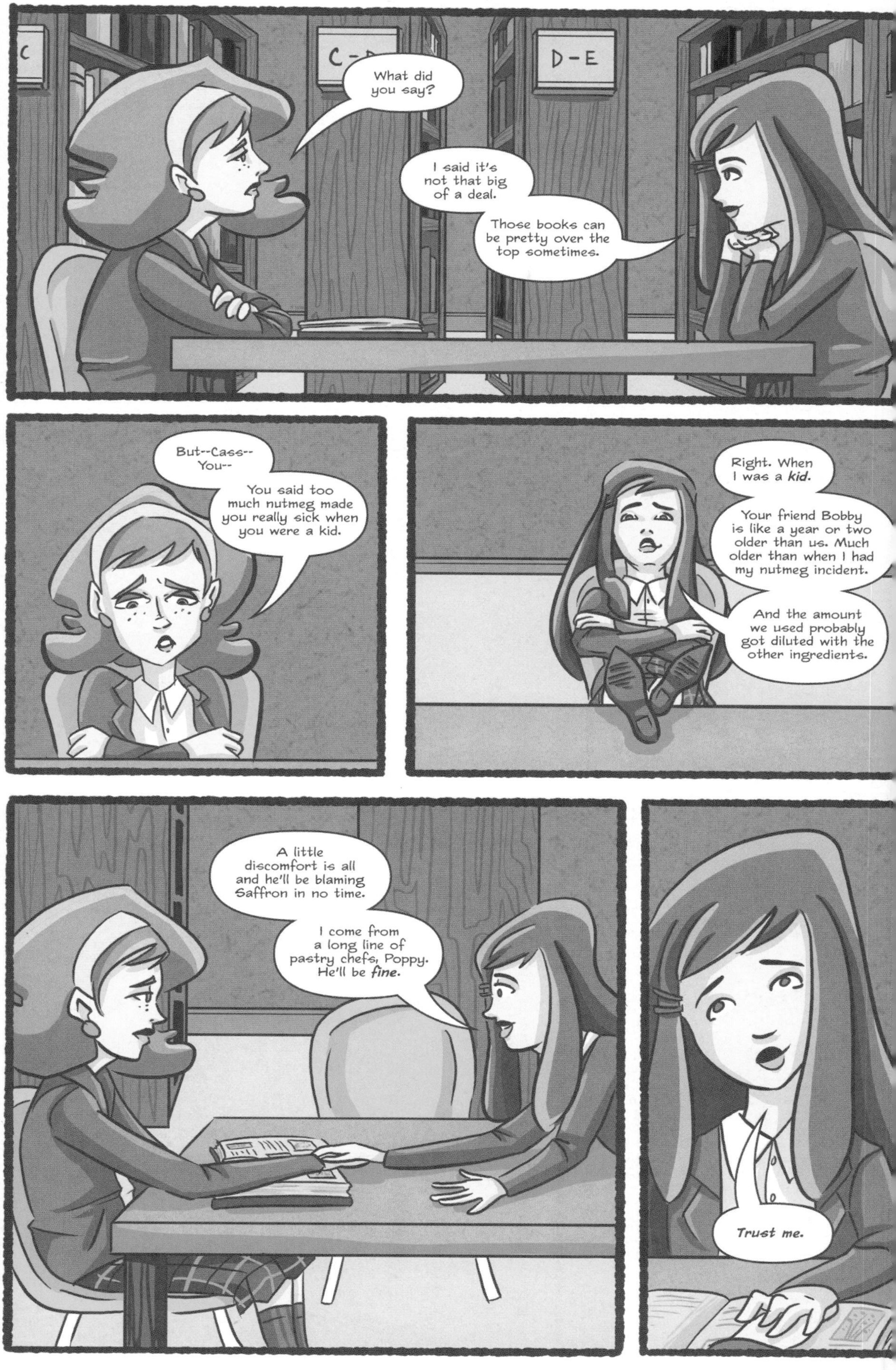
C
C-D
D-E
What did you say?
I said it's not that big of a deal.
Those books can be pretty over the top sometimes.
But--Cass-- You--
You said too much nutmeg made you really sick when you were a kid.
Right. When I was a *kid.*
Your friend Bobby is like a year or two older than us. Much older than when I had my nutmeg incident.
And the amount we used probably got diluted with the other ingredients.
A little discomfort is all and he'll be blaming Saffron in no time.
I come from a long line of pastry chefs, Poppy. He'll be *fine.*
Trust me.

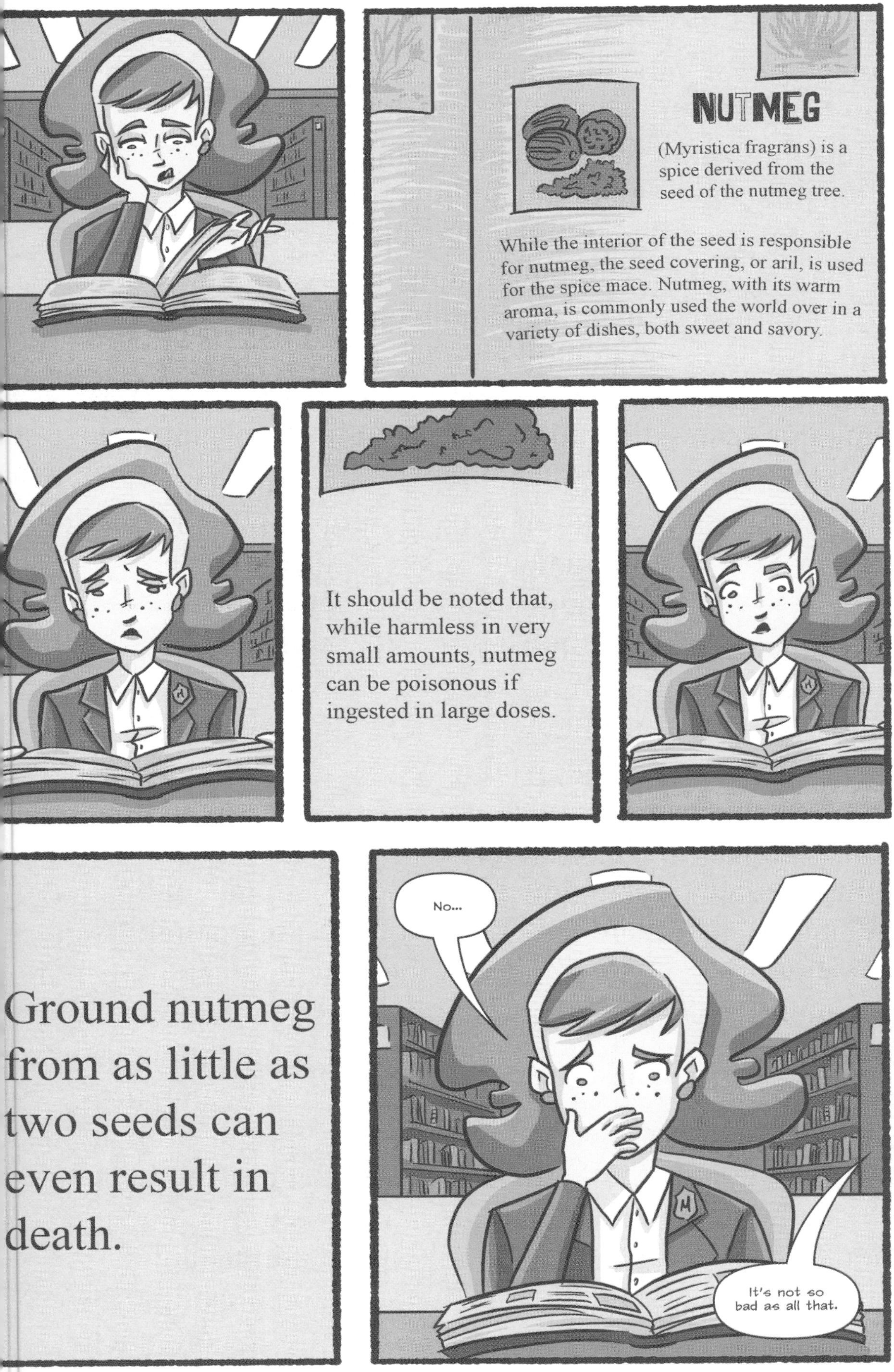
NUTMEG
(Myristica fragrans) is a spice derived from the seed of the nutmeg tree.
While the interior of the seed is responsible for nutmeg, the seed covering, or aril, is used for the spice mace. Nutmeg, with its warm aroma, is commonly used the world over in a variety of dishes, both sweet and savory.
It should be noted that, while harmless in very small amounts, nutmeg can be poisonous if ingested in large doses.
Ground nutmeg from as little as two seeds can even result in death.
No...
It's not so bad as all that.

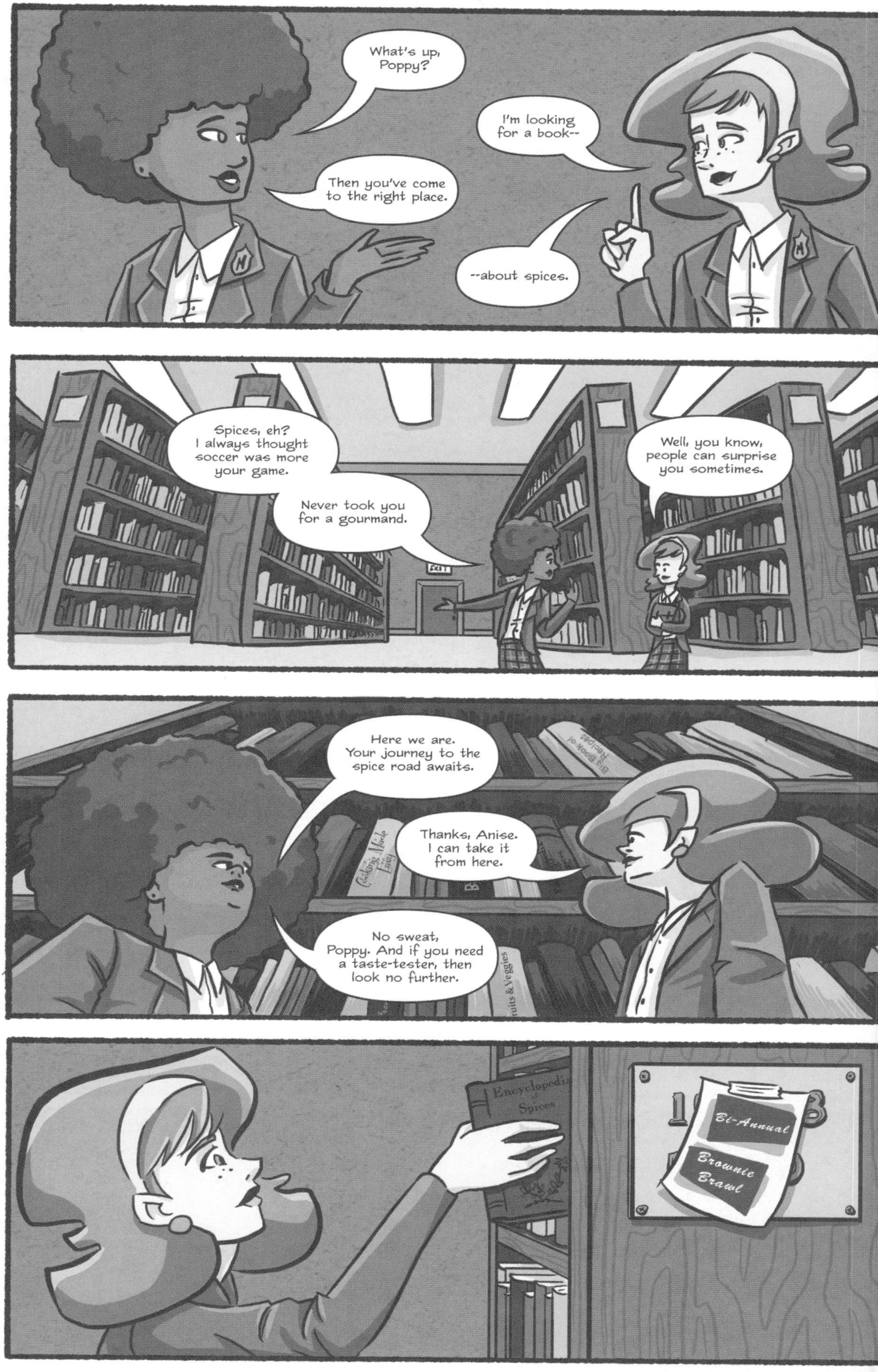
What's up, Poppy?
I'm looking for a book--
Then you've come to the right place.
--about spices.
Spices, eh? I always thought soccer was more your game.
Never took you for a gourmand.
EXIT
Well, you know, people can surprise you sometimes.
Here we are. Your journey to the spice road awaits.
Big Book of Recipes
Cooking Made Easy
Thanks, Anise. I can take it from here.
No sweat, Poppy. And if you need a taste-tester, then look no further.
Bi-Annual
Brownie Brawl

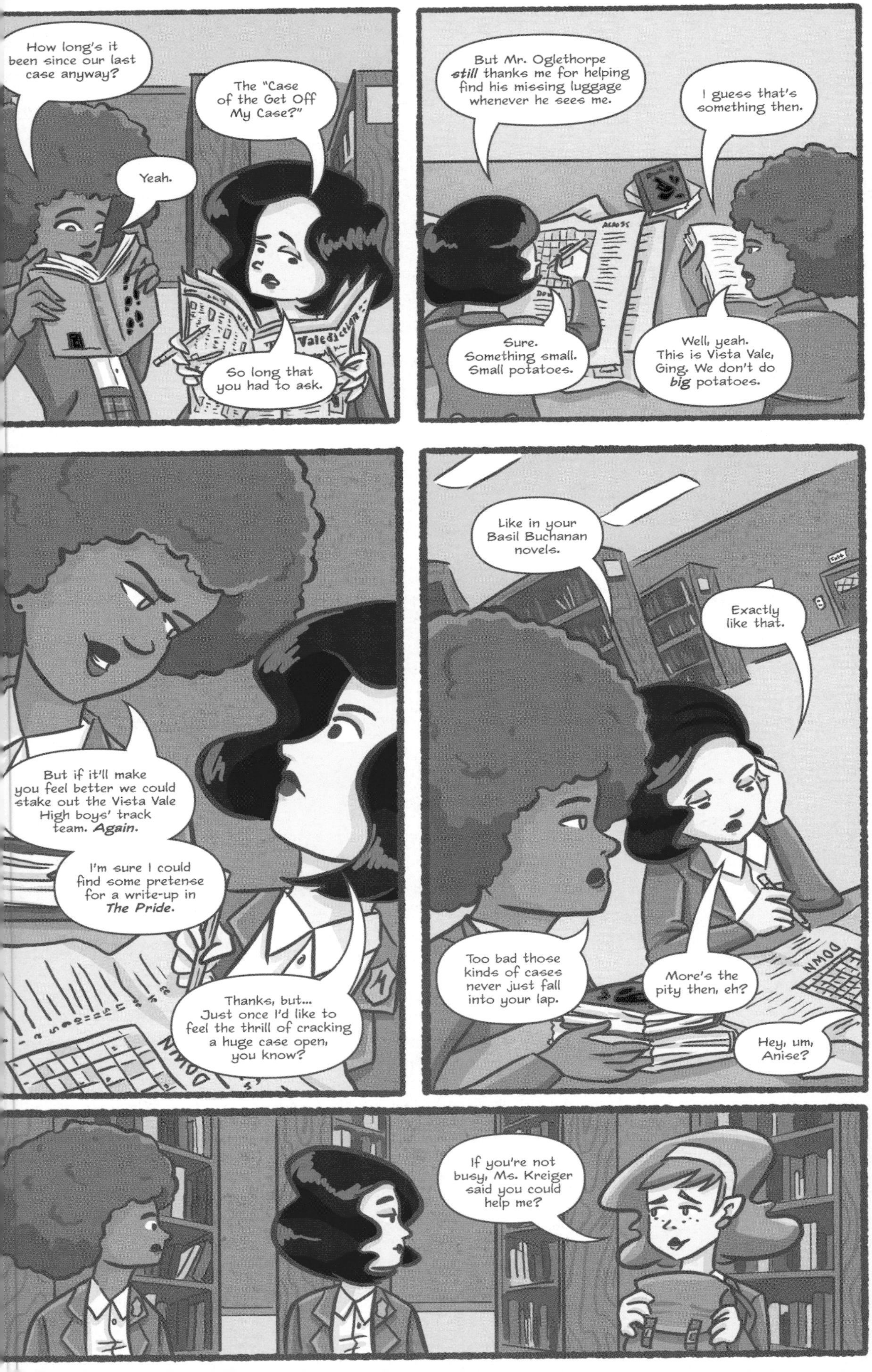
How long's it been since our last case anyway?
The "Case of the Get Off My Case?"
Yeah.
So long that you had to ask.
But Mr. Oglethorpe *still* thanks me for helping find his missing luggage whenever he sees me.
I guess that's something then.
Sure. Something small. Small potatoes.
Well, yeah. This is Vista Vale, Ging. We don't do *big* potatoes.
But if it'll make you feel better we could stake out the Vista Vale High boys' track team. *Again.*
I'm sure I could find some pretense for a write-up in *The Pride.*
Thanks, but... Just once I'd like to feel the thrill of cracking a huge case open, you know?
Like in your Basil Buchanan novels.
Exactly like that.
Too bad those kinds of cases never just fall into your lap.
More's the pity then, eh?
Hey, um, Anise?
If you're not busy, Ms. Kreiger said you could help me?

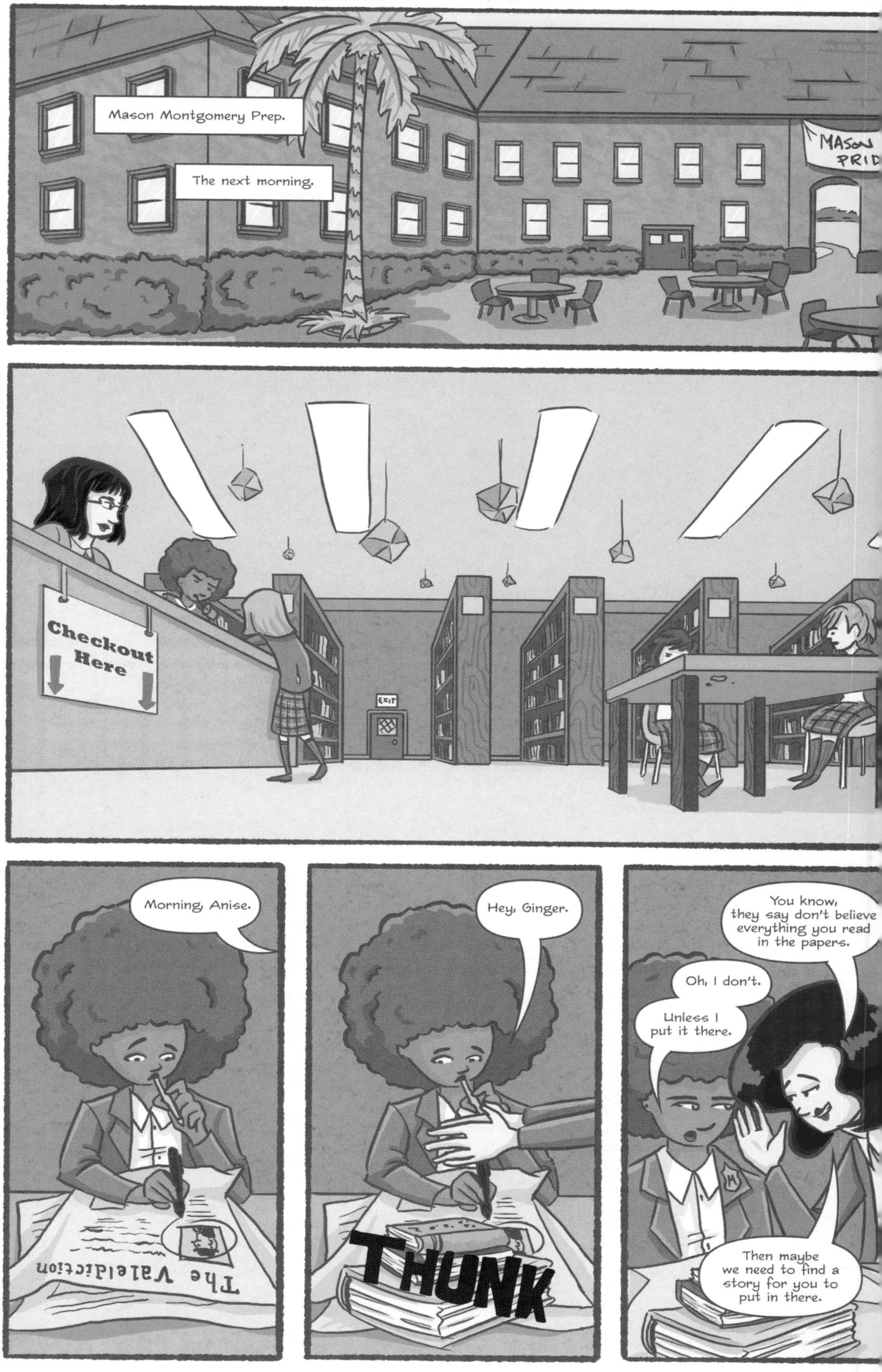

Mason Montgomery Prep.
The next morning.
MASON PRID
Checkout Here
EXIT
Morning, Anise.
The Valediction
Hey, Ginger.
THUNK
You know, they say don't believe everything you read in the papers.
Oh, I don't.
Unless I put it there.
Then maybe we need to find a story for you to put in there.

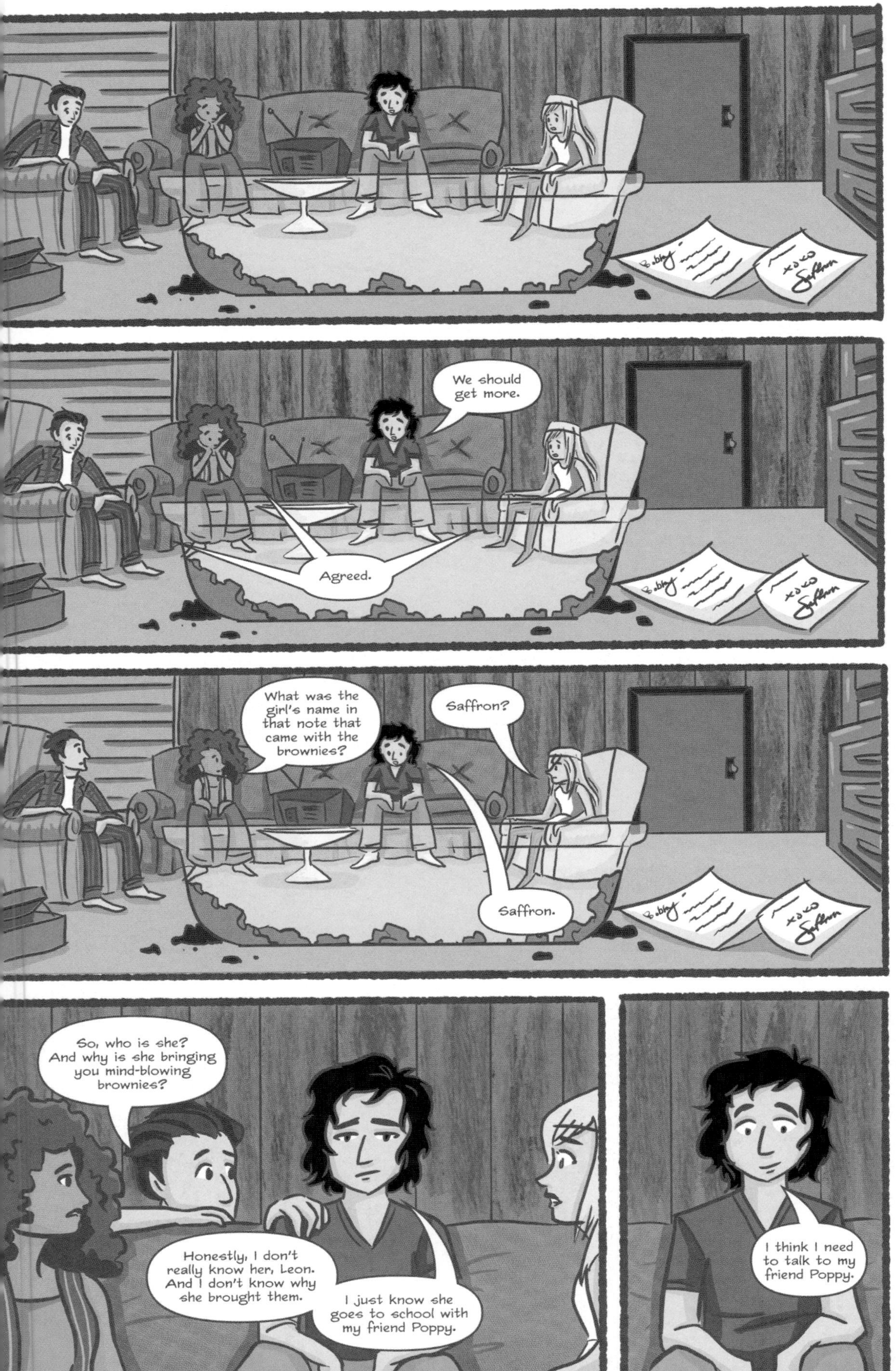
We should get more.
Agreed.
What was the girl's name in that note that came with the brownies?
Saffron?
Saffron.
So, who is she? And why is she bringing you mind-blowing brownies?
Honestly, I don't really know her, Leon. And I don't know why she brought them.
I just know she goes to school with my friend Poppy.
I think I need to talk to my friend Poppy.

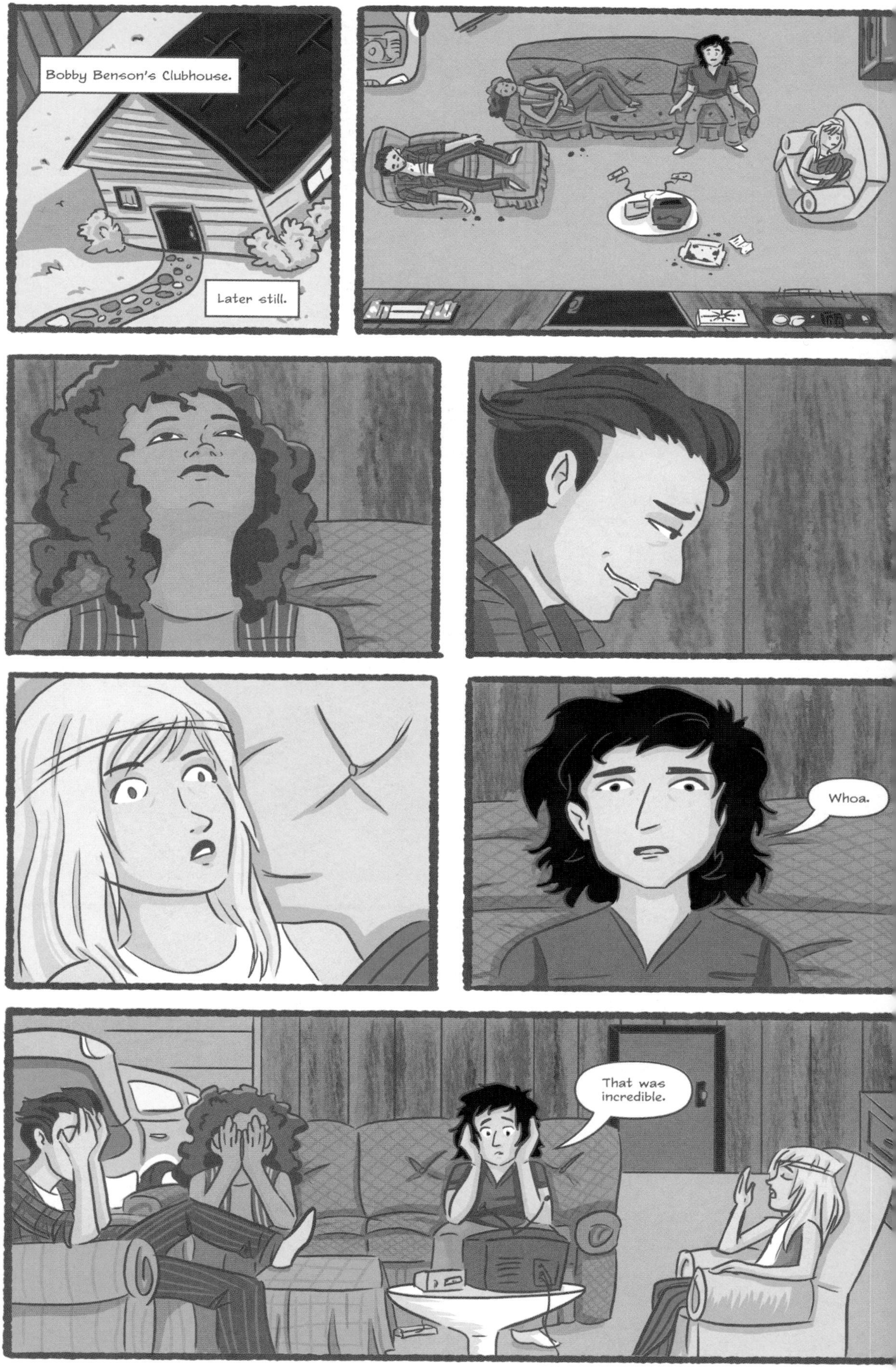
Bobby Benson's Clubhouse.
Later still.
Whoa.
That was incredible.

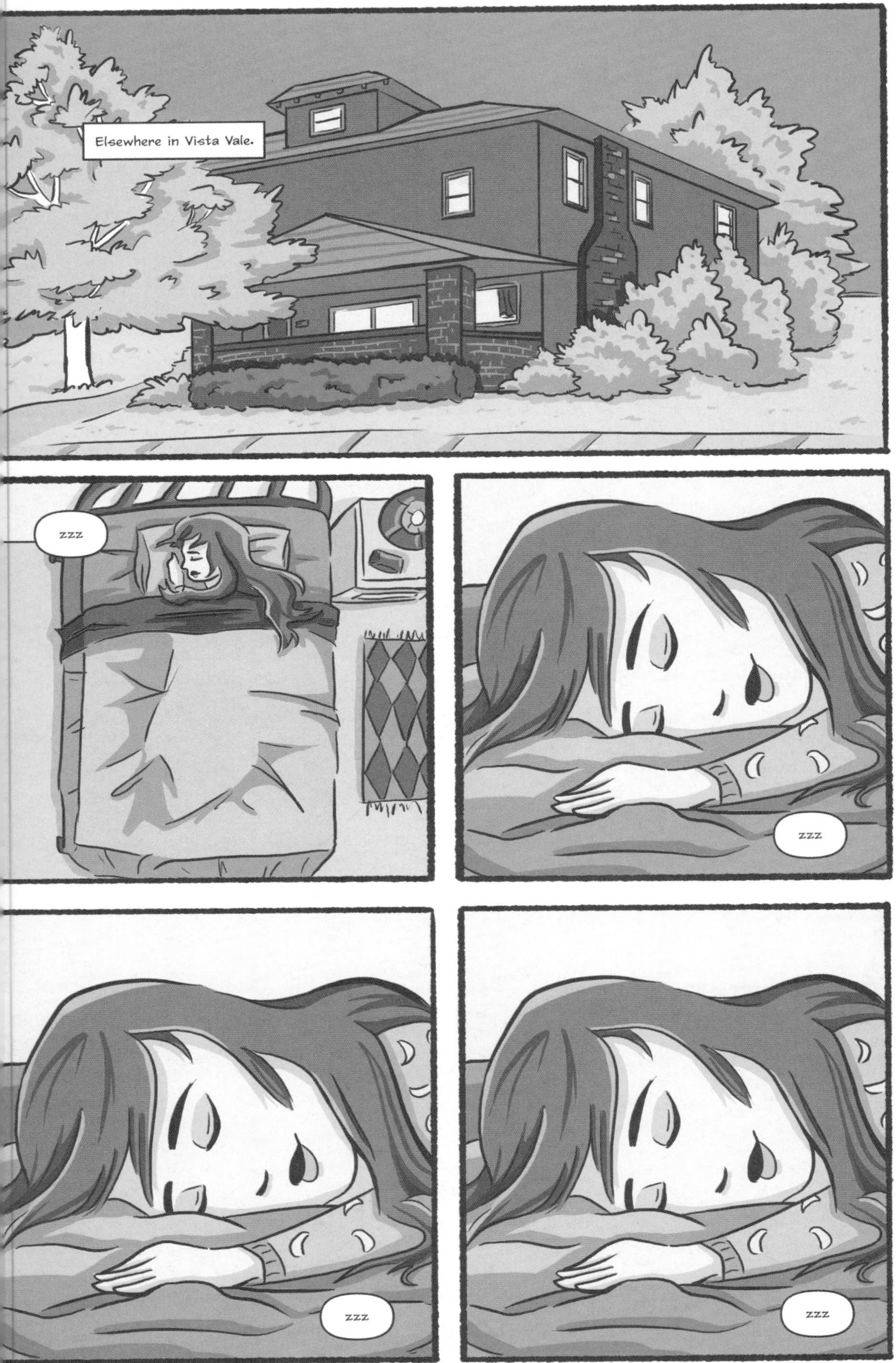
Elsewhere in Vista Vale.
zzz
zzz
zzz
zzz

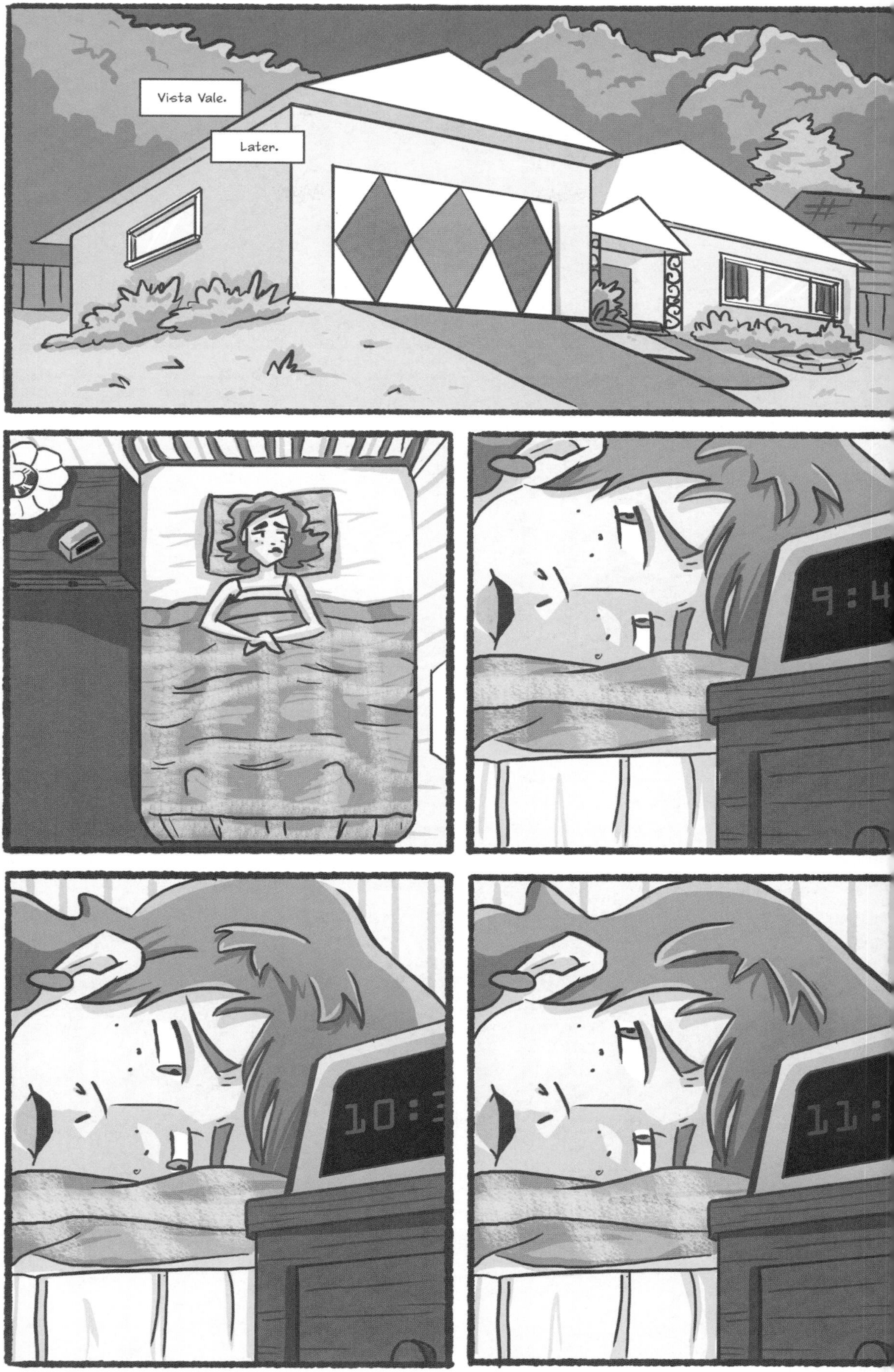
Vista Vale.
Later.

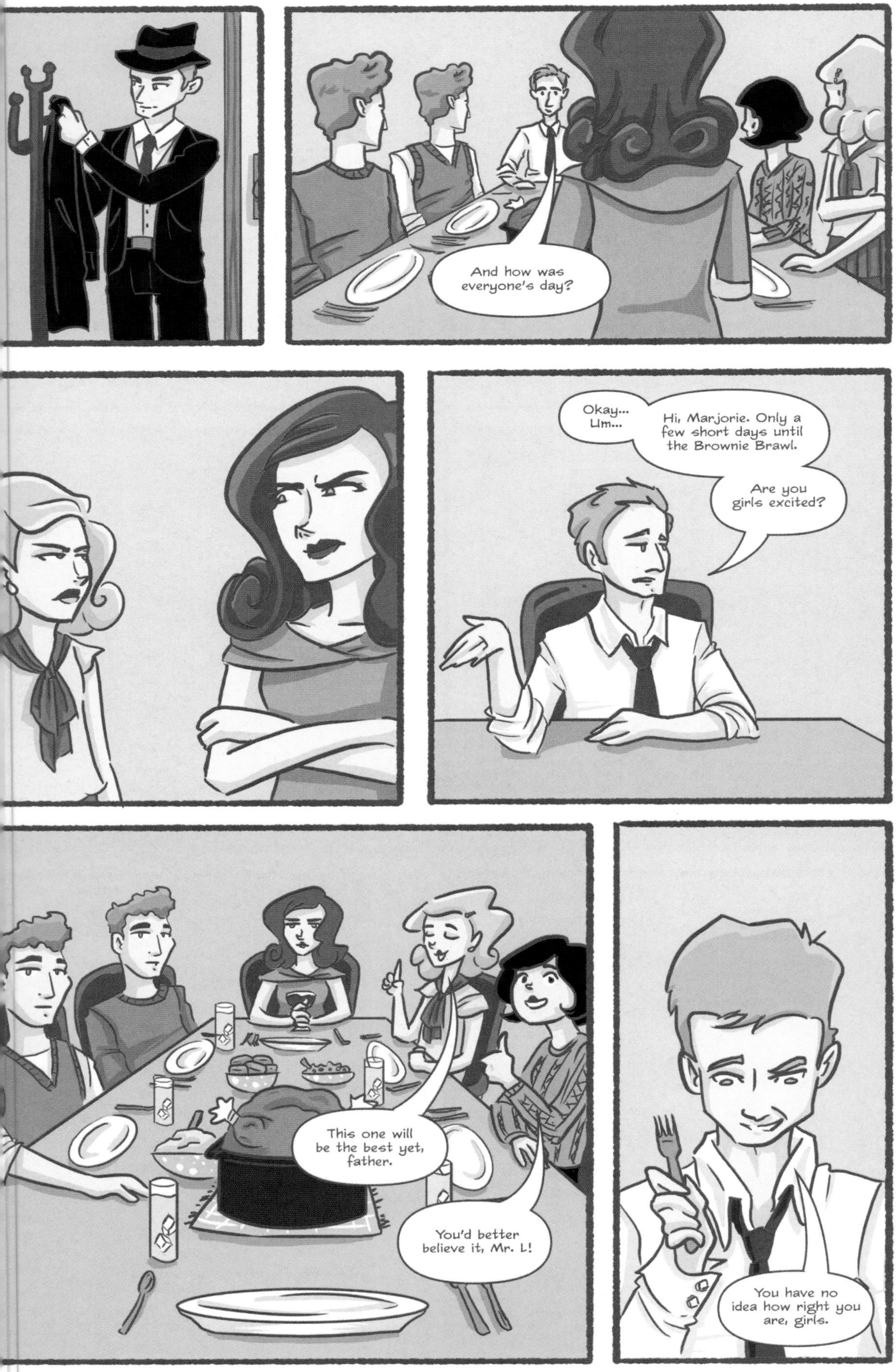
And how was everyone's day?
Okay... Um...
Hi, Marjorie. Only a few short days until the Brownie Brawl.
Are you girls excited?
This one will be the best yet, father.
You'd better believe it, Mr. L!
You have no idea how right you are, girls.

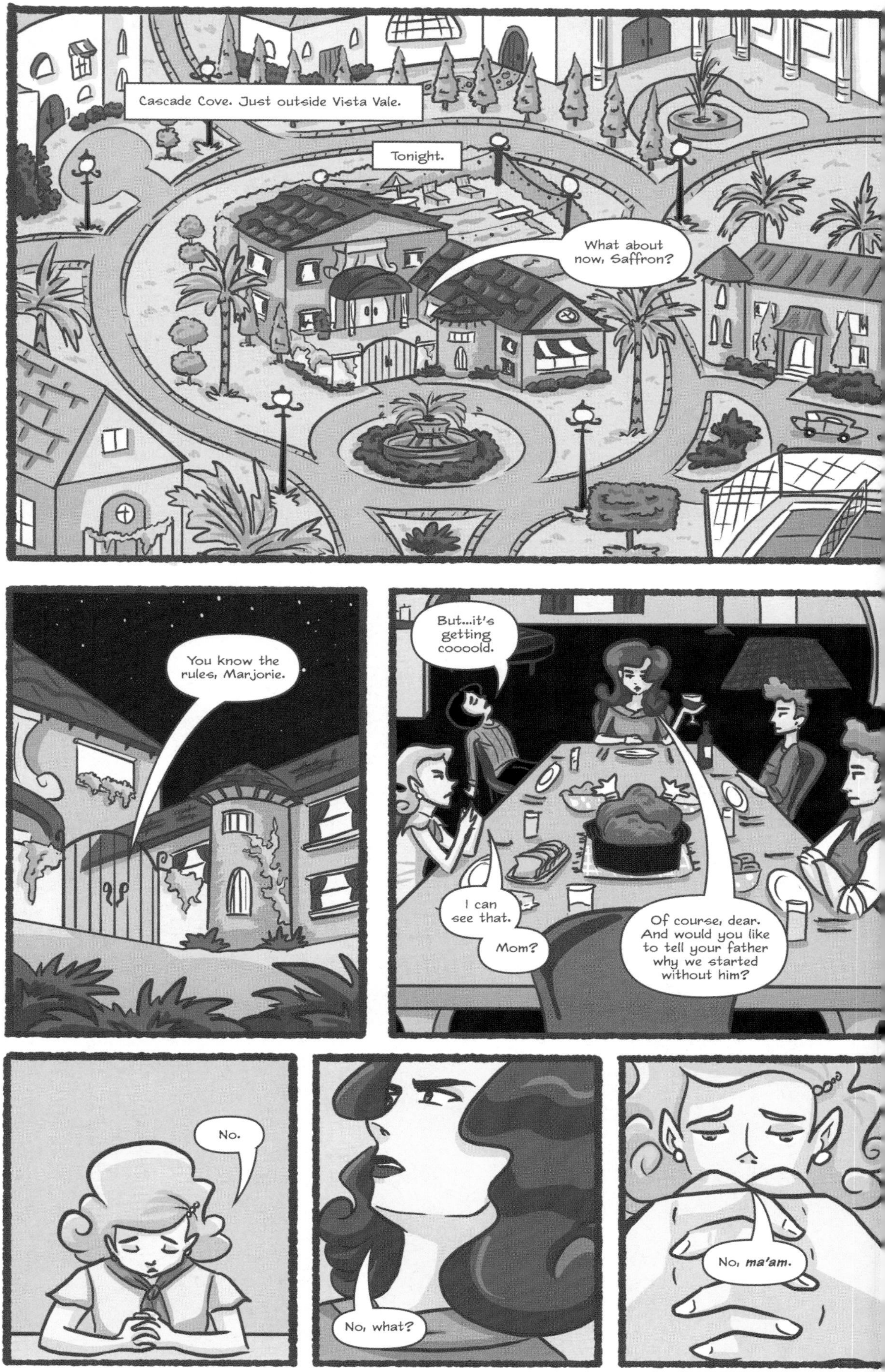
Cascade Cove. Just outside Vista Vale.
Tonight.
What about now, Saffron?
You know the rules, Marjorie.
But...it's getting coooold.
I can see that.
Mom?
Of course, dear. And would you like to tell your father why we started without him?
No.
No, what?
No, *ma'am*.

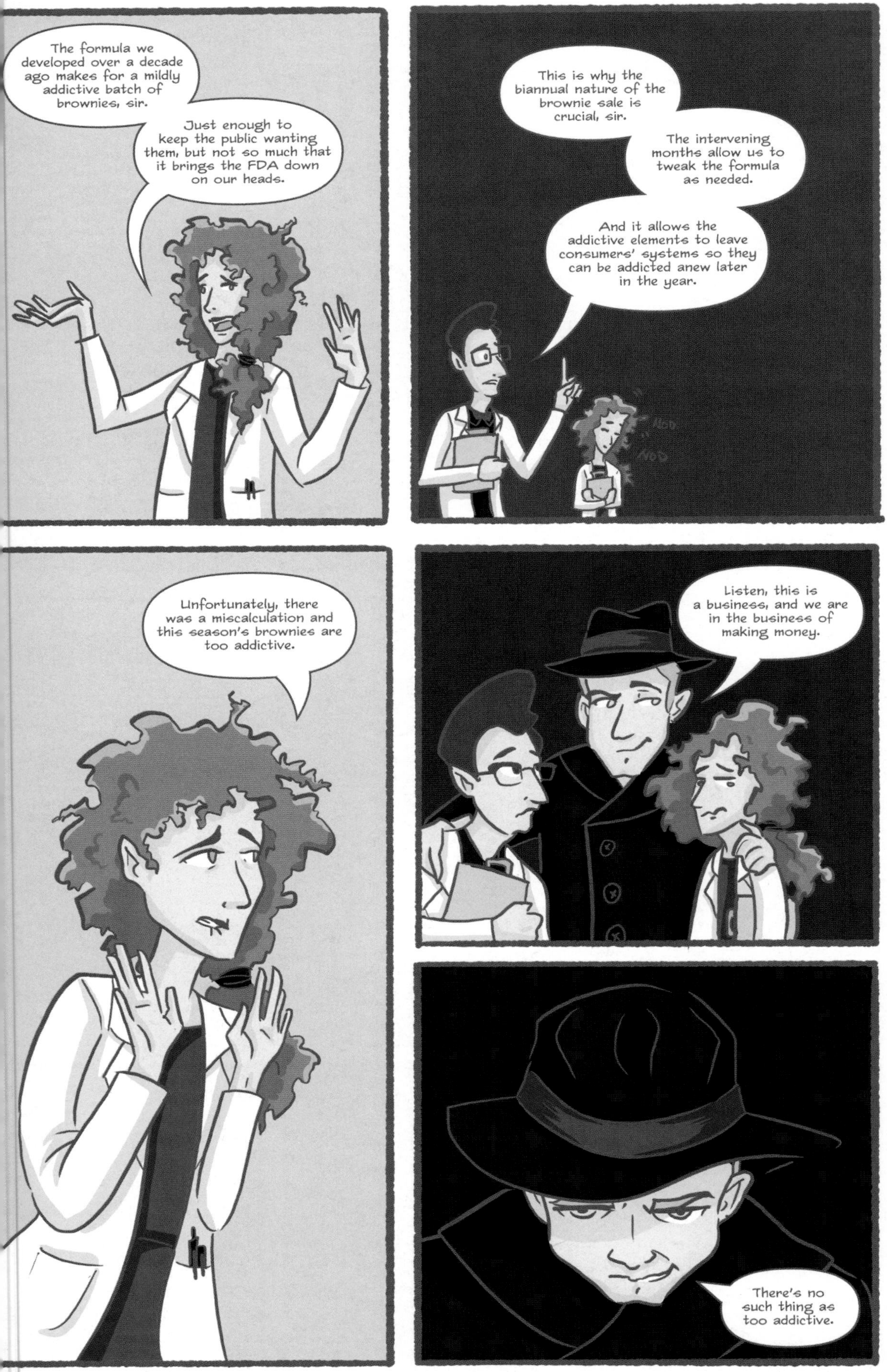
The formula we developed over a decade ago makes for a mildly addictive batch of brownies, sir.
Just enough to keep the public wanting them, but not so much that it brings the FDA down on our heads.
This is why the biannual nature of the brownie sale is crucial, sir.
The intervening months allow us to tweak the formula as needed.
And it allows the addictive elements to leave consumers' systems so they can be addicted anew later in the year.
NOD
NOD
Unfortunately, there was a miscalculation and this season's brownies are too addictive.
Listen, this is a business, and we are in the business of making money.
There's no such thing as too addictive.

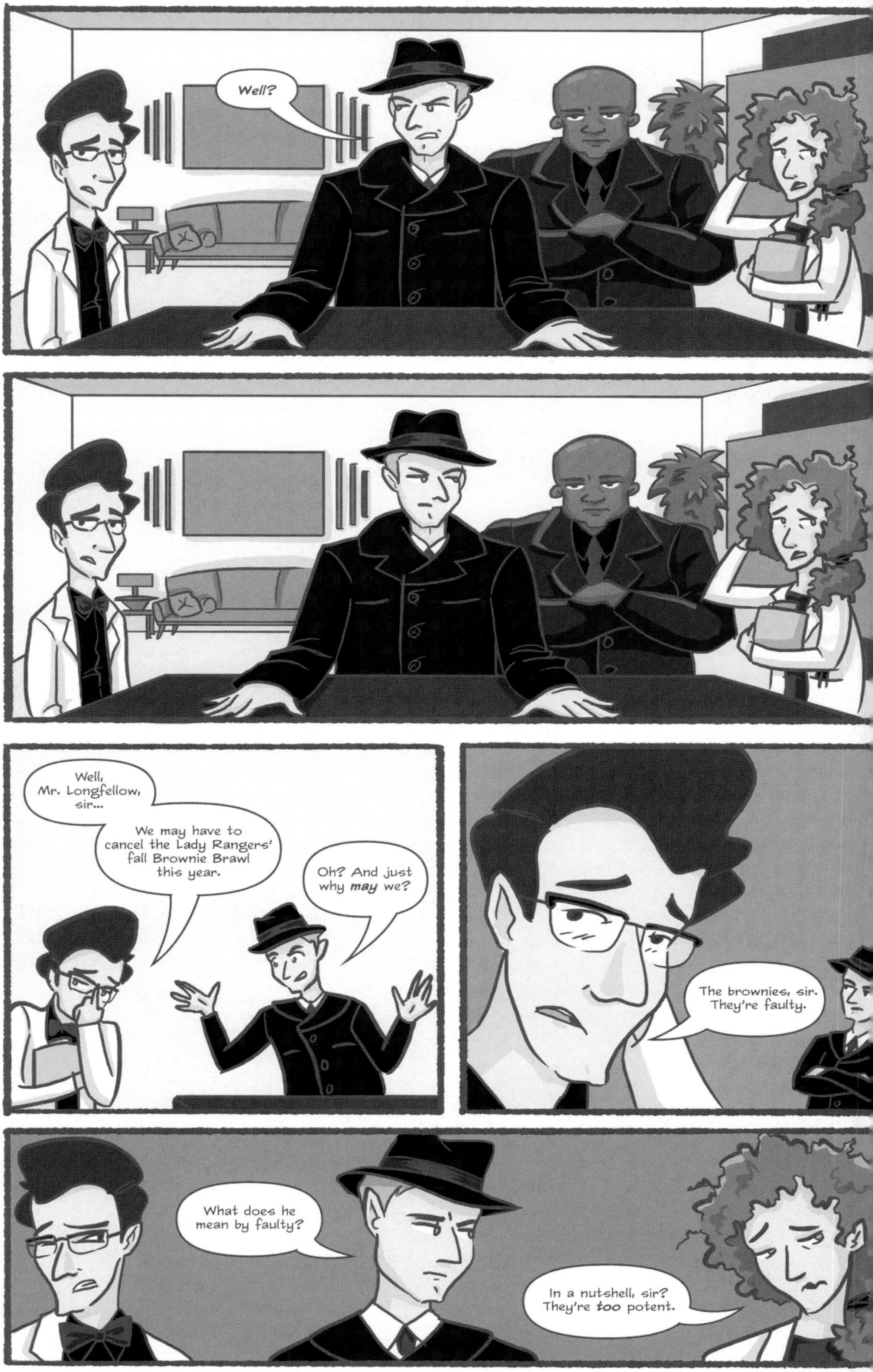
Well?
Well, Mr. Longfellow, sir...
We may have to cancel the Lady Rangers' fall Brownie Brawl this year.
Oh? And just why *may* we?
The brownies, sir. They're faulty.
What does he mean by faulty?
In a nutshell, sir? They're *too* potent.

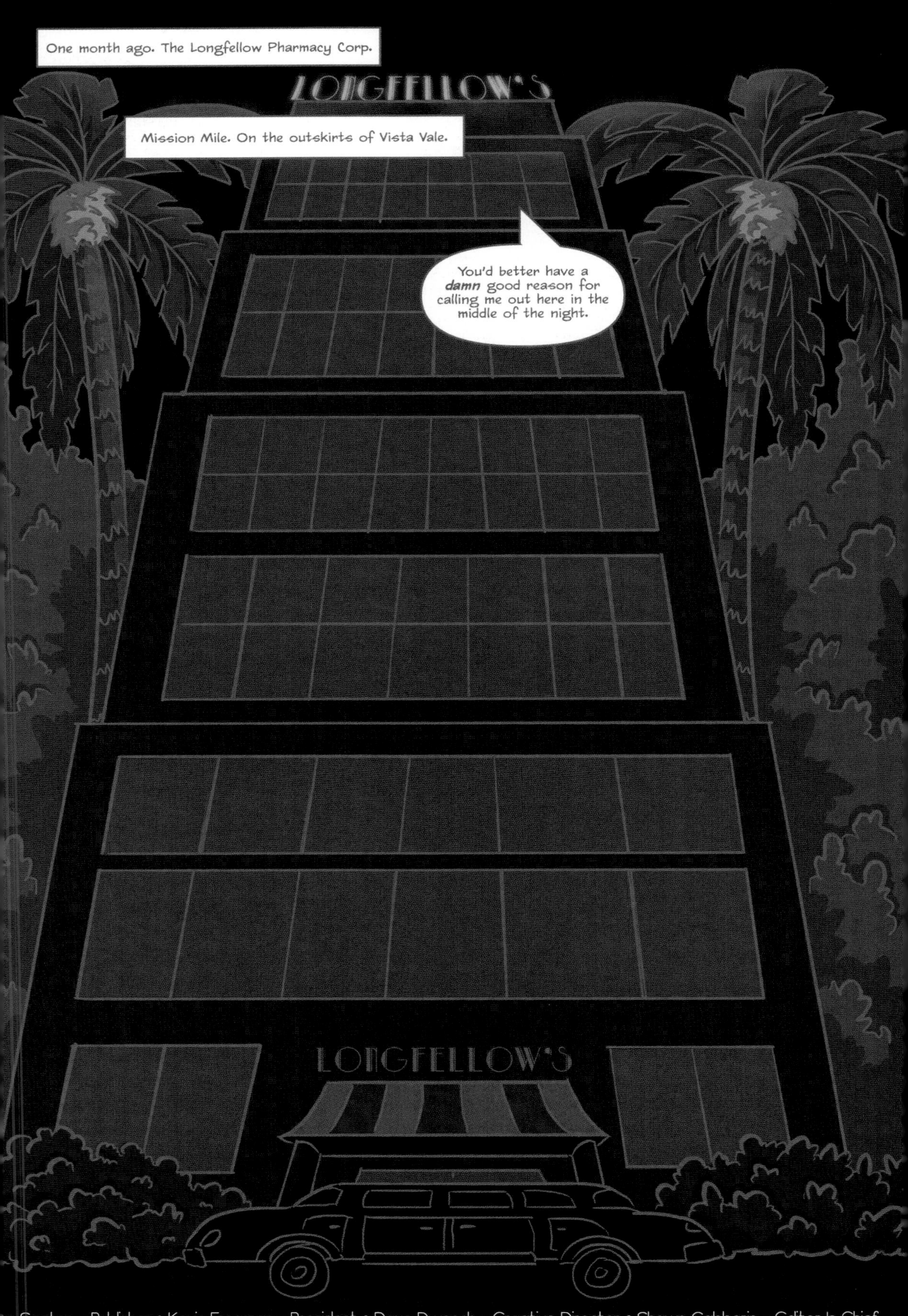
One month ago. The Longfellow Pharmacy Corp.
LONGFELLOW'S
Mission Mile. On the outskirts of Vista Vale.
You'd better have a *damn* good reason for calling me out here in the middle of the night.
LONGFELLOW'S

an Seaton - Publisher • Kevin Freeman - President • Dave Dwonch - Creative Director • Shawn Gabborin - Editor In Chief
al Igle & Kelly Dale- Co-Directors of Marketing • Social Media Director - Jim Dietz • Education Outreach Director - Jeremy Whitley
Chad Cicconi - ate all the brownies • Colleen Boyd - Associate Editor

THE ADVENTURES OF
AERO-GiRL

AVAILABLE IN FINER STORES EVERYWHE

s Aero-Girl, Jacqueline Mackenzie is the protector of Foxbay. As the sidekick to Battle Ja
er father, her life couldn't be any better; but tragedy is just around the corner! Will she b
ready to defend her city against the evil of Dr. Chimera and his army of AniMen? Can
Aero-Girl be the hero she (and her father) always dreamed of being?

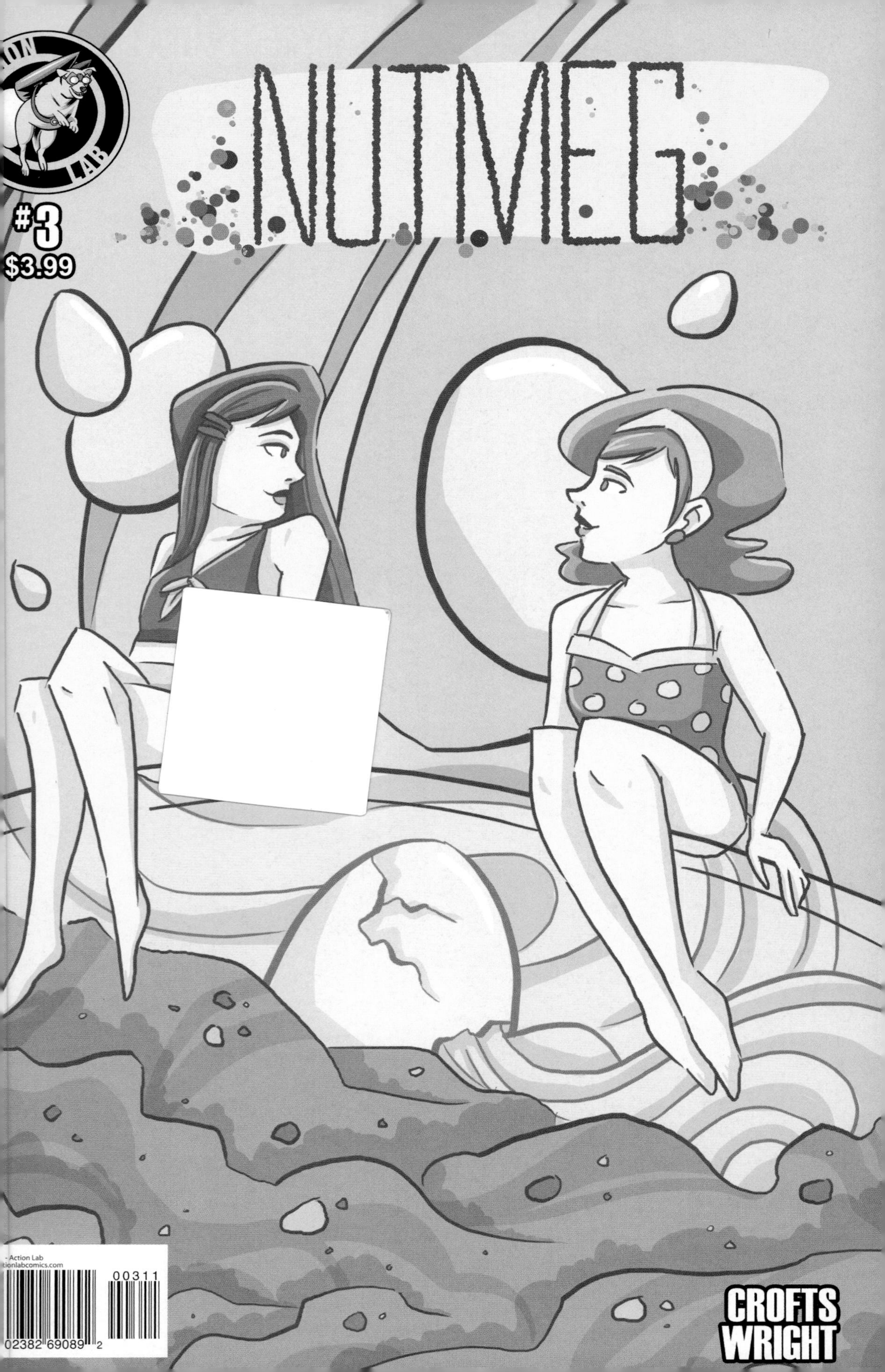
NUTMEG
#3
$3.99
CROFTS
WRIGHT

ACTION LAB

READ MORE NOW

Nutmeg - Action Lab
www.actionlabcomics.com
00211
7 02382 69089 2

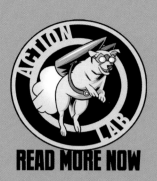

ACTIONLABCOMICS.COM

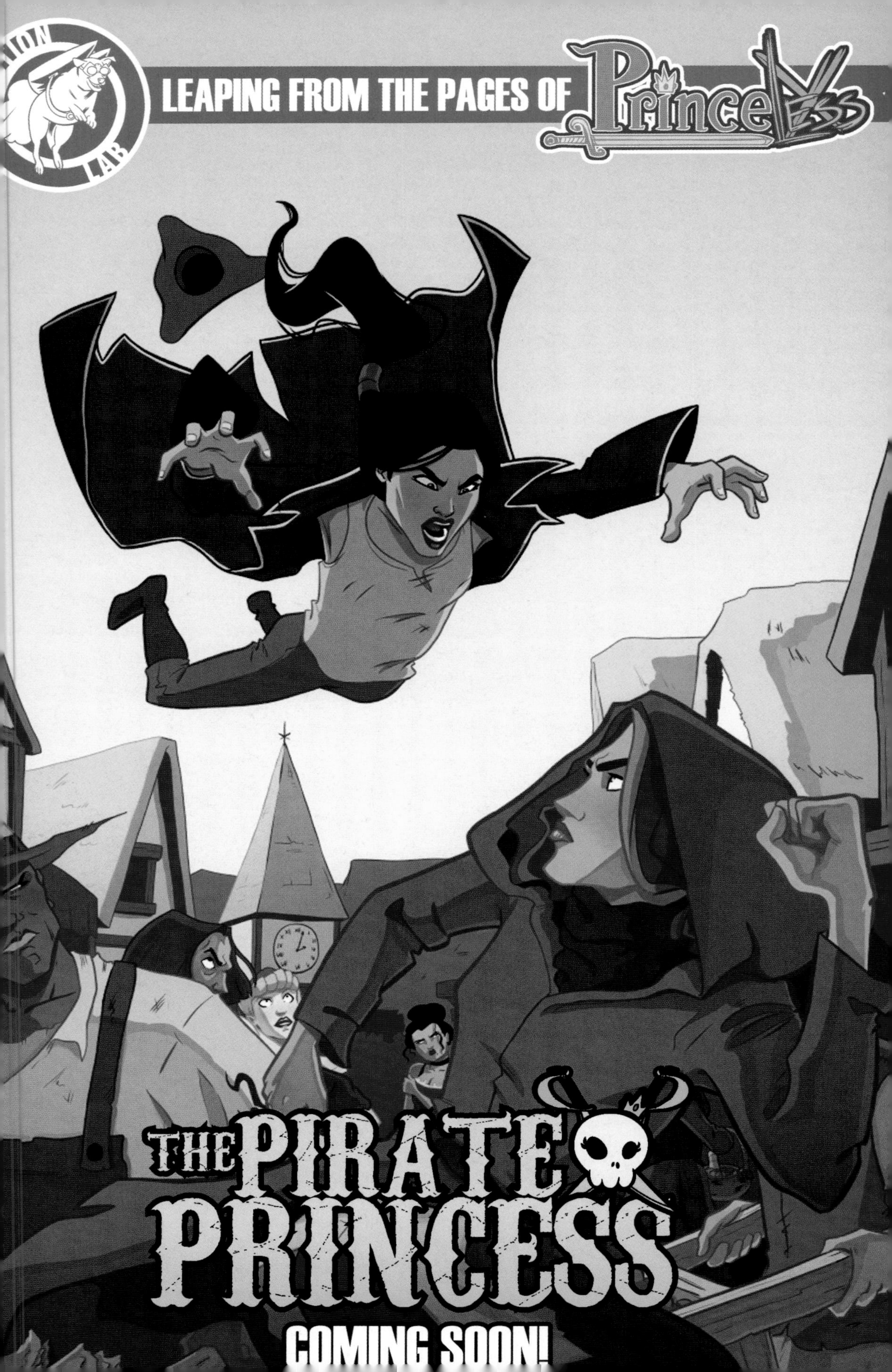
LEAPING FROM THE PAGES OF
Princeless
THE PIRATE PRINCESS
COMING SOON!

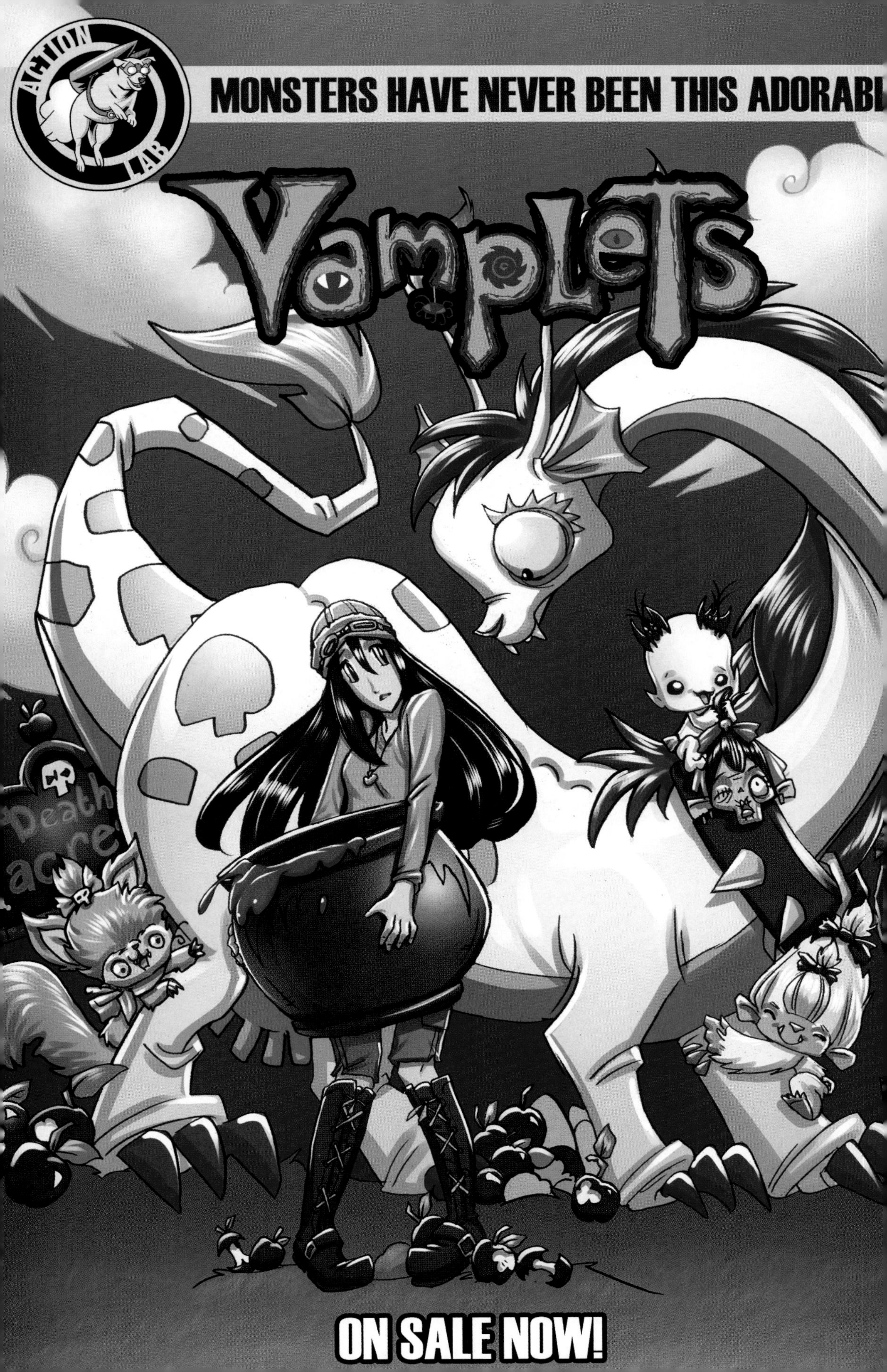
ACTION LAB
MONSTERS HAVE NEVER BEEN THIS ADORABL
VAMPLETS
Death acre
ON SALE NOW!

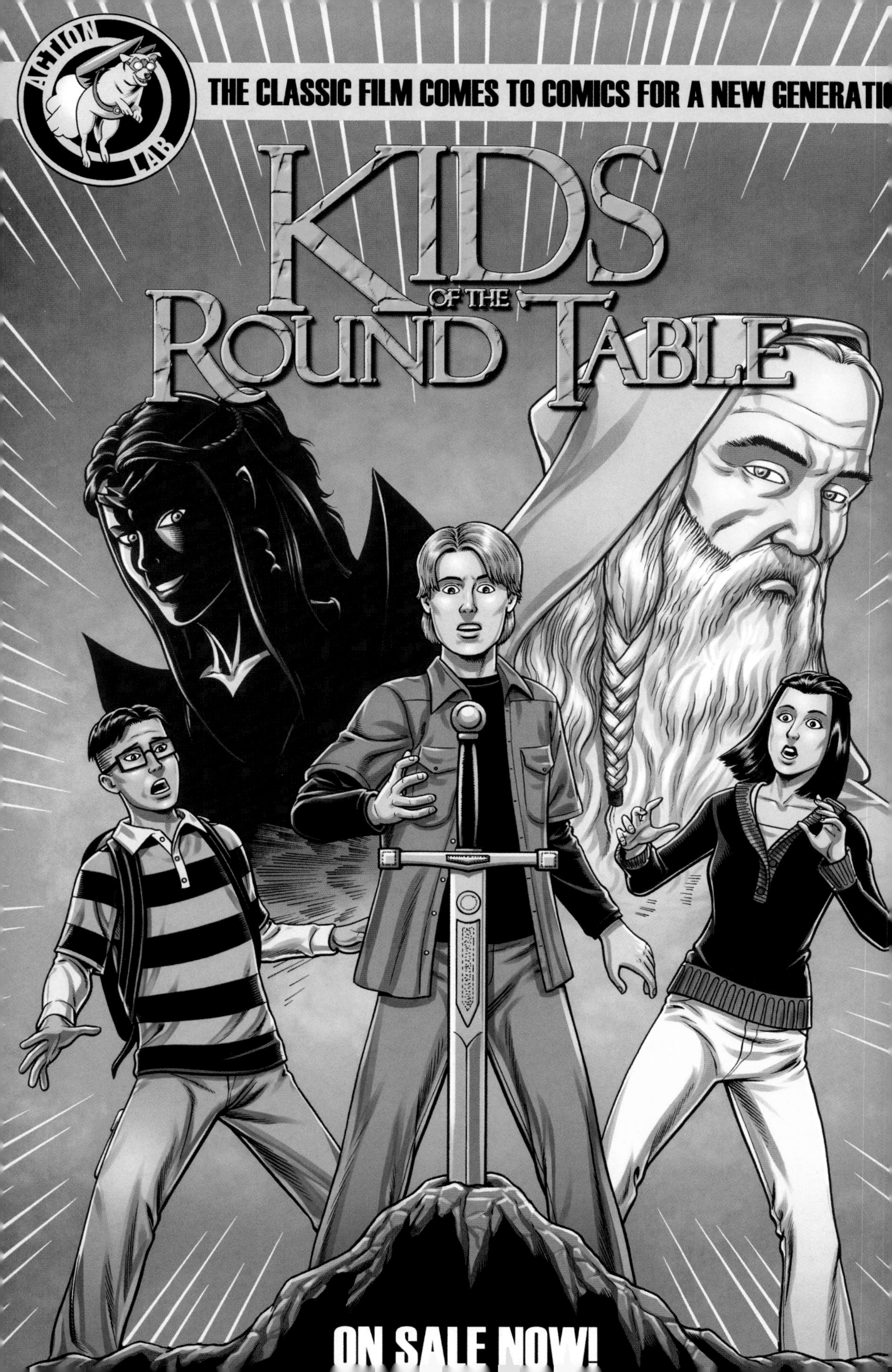
ACTION LAB
THE CLASSIC FILM COMES TO COMICS FOR A NEW GENERATI
KIDS OF THE ROUND TABLE
ON SALE NOW!

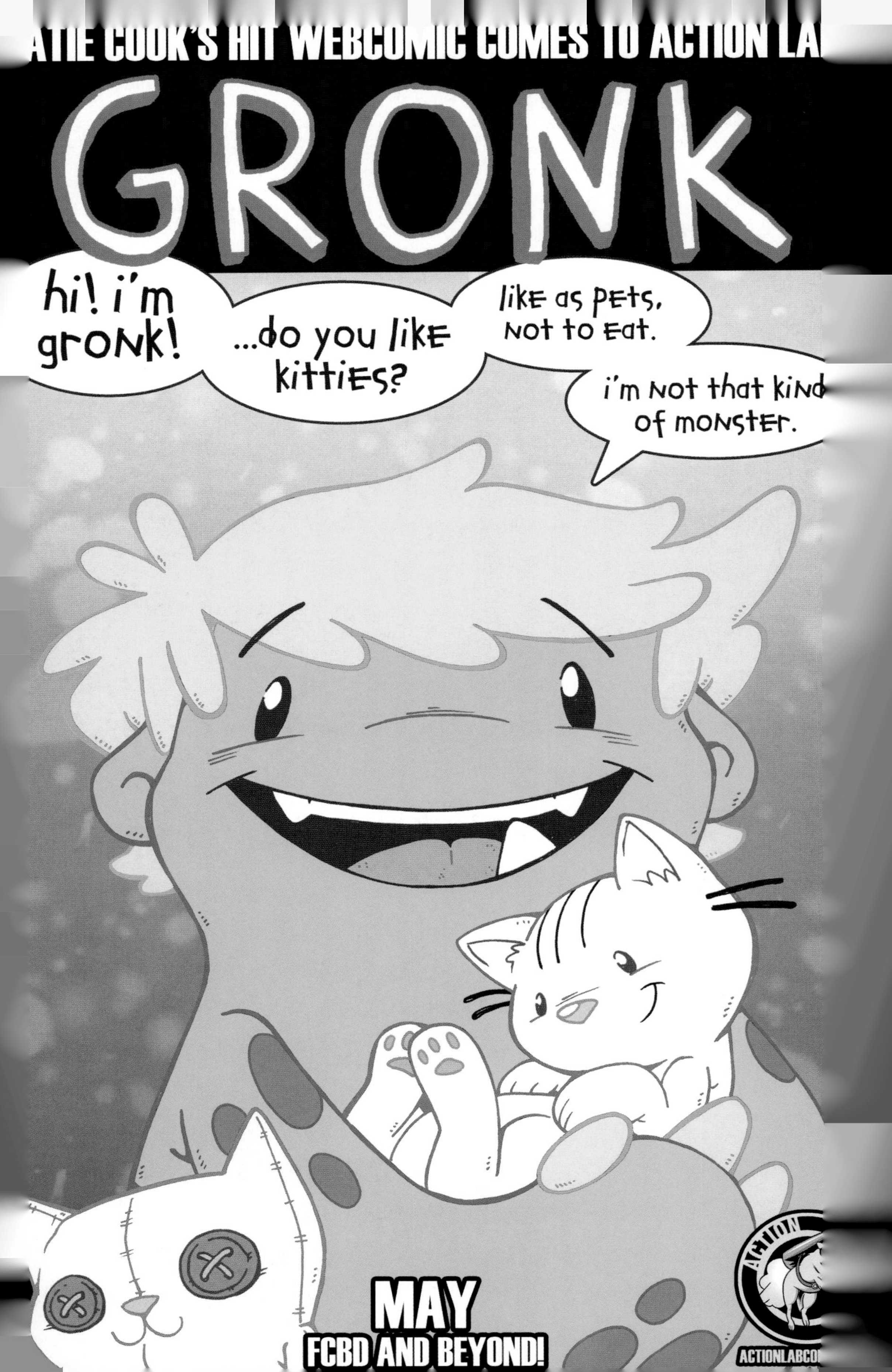
ATIE COOK'S HIT WEBCOMIC COMES TO ACTION LA
GRONK
hi! i'm gronk!
...do you like kitties?
like as pets, not to eat.
i'm not that kind of monster.
MAY
FCBD AND BEYOND!

Preheat your oven to 350F. Lightly grease a 9x13 pan or use parchment paper . Pro tip, scrunch up the parchment paper first like your balling up a piece of newspaper then smooth it out before laying it in the pan. It'll lay flatter for you and give you less drama when you're pouring in your batter.

Sift flour, baking powder, and salt and set aside. Sifters are usually terrible so I usually just use one of those mesh strainers. They're messier, but faster.

In another larger bowl, beat together butter, brown sugar, eggs and vanilla until smooth. If your butter is soft enough, you can use a spoon. Baking should not require advance technology, no matter what the tyrannical owners of fancy stand mixers say.

Slowly combine the dry ingredients with the wet ones until smooth and all mixed in. It's gonna look a lot like cookie batter. When all combined, pour the batter into your prepared pan. It's gonna be kinda sticky so you'll need to scoop it out and spread it evenly to all the corners.

Combine the white sugar and pumpkin pie spice in a small bowl, then sprinkle the mixture directly on top of the batter. Make sure every bit is covered evenly. And don't worry if you have extra topping left.

FYI, when November hits and everyone won't shut up about pumpkin flavored everything, what they actually want is pumpkin pie spice. And it's actually really versatile. I use it for almost everything that calls for cinnamon. But not all blends you find in the store are made equal. Try to find one with cardamom in it. Those are my favorite.

Put your brownies in the oven for 25-30 minutes or until the top sorta springs back into place when you touch it with your finger or the back of a spoon. Let it cool for like 10 minutes in the pan, then cut the brownies while their still a little hot.

And if you're feeling really sassy, top that with some vanilla ice cream. Trust me, it'll blow your mind.

For whatever the occasion, whether you're making them for a party or for a party of one featuring you, your couch fort, and your Netflix account. Enjoy.

Your friend in the fire,

Katie Kruger

Hello there *Nutmeg* readers!

So I've been asked to share one of my favorite recipes here on The Cooling Rack but first, let's talk about why people cook.

People use food for all kinds of reasons, the most boring of which is to make sure you stay alive. Food can be just as expressive and beautiful as a work of art and can be used for so many things. You can show love, you can eat your feelings, impress your friends, or seek revenge on your enemies (wink). Me, I'm a stress baker and a people pleaser. If I'm feeling like the world is spinning on the wrong axis and things have gone just a bit pear shaped, nothing soothes the nerves like baking. Did some creepy dude on the street start shouting at me? Make some cookies. Did I get a bad grade on a test? What a perfect time to make a cake.

The world outside my kitchen is chaotic and unfair. Sometimes, most times, even when you do everything exactly as your told, follow all the rules, and do everything "correctly," things can still get mucked up and bad. Such is not true with baking. There are rules that have to be followed, measurements that must be taken precisely and if you follow the path laid out for you, you almost always end up with something yummy. Plus, the end result can be given away and you can hear my favorite sound in the world—the involuntary YUUUMMM noise. You know, that moment right after a person takes a bite of something you made where they pause, take a breath, and just yuuummmmmm.

That yum gives me goosebumps. I go out of my way to make that yum noise come out of people's faces. So without further ado, I give you my recipe for Snickerdoodle Brownies. A guaranteed stress reliever and yum maker that is both easy and way impressive.

Snickerdoodle Brownies

Adapted from DozenFlours.com

2 2/3 cups all purpose flour

2 tsp baking powder

1 tsp salt

2 cups packed brown sugar

3/4 cup unsalted butter (1 ½ sticks) , at room temperature

2 large eggs

2 tbsp vanilla

2 tbsp white sugar

2 tsp pumpkin pie spice

So how in the world does a film like this—as tragic as it reveals itself to be—influence something like *Nutmeg*?

Well, once I knew *Nutmeg* was going to be a crime story featuring teenage girls--the original idea was a story told from the perspective of Nancy Drew's nemeses--I knew *Heavenly Creatures* would factor into it somewhere. In fact, the first few pages of *Nutmeg #1* mirror the early bits of Peter Jackson's film. The strong-willed Cassia Caraway's arrival at Mason Montgomery Prep, and her teaming with the more reserved Poppy Pepper signals a shift in the order of things among the girls in Vista Vale. Poppy provides a guide for Cassia to understand and navigate the school and community, while Cassia gives Poppy a fearless confidante and ally in her day-to-day dealings at school.

One of the ways *Nutmeg* differs, though, is that it's the series' primary antagonist, the monied Saffron Longfellow, leader of the Lady Rangers, who drives the two girls together. Saffron serves as the catalyst for Poppy and Cassia's friendship, once Poppy sees new girl Cassia stand up to Saffron on her very first day of school. In *Heavenly Creatures* the antagonism comes from Pauline and Juliet's parents, fearful of the intensity of the girls' friendship and what it could mean. That being said, both stories find at their hearts two girls adrift in adolescence and latching on to one another for survival.

It's important for me to note as well that while *Nutmeg* does (or will) have its own share of tragedies, they never reach the enormity of what's depicted in *Heavenly Creatures*, not the least because the latter is based on actual events. For Poppy and Cassia in *Nutmeg*, their turn toward criminality is borne of their need to assert their perceived superiority over the established order of teenagers, and to create for themselves a sense of control in their own lives.

Among the many things I've enjoyed in working on *Nutmeg* is seeing Jackie's art as we progress. I knew from the moment I saw her character designs that it was going to be something special. Her style, from the girls' hairstyles to the softer pastel coloring to the Vista Vale town center, evokes the same sort of idyllic world as *Heavenly Creatures*' Christchurch. The sort of place where crime supposedly never happens, and when it does it is shocking and tragic. In fact, it's that very softness in Jackie's art that most effectively contrasts the darker-but-not-too-dark criminal elements that seep into the story. In that respect it's visually somewhere between cozy mystery and film soleil.

The trope of the teen detective has been effective and apparent in everything from the *Scooby-Doo* gang to Rian Johnson's fantastic film *Brick*, but *Heavenly Creatures*, told solely from the perspective of the perpetrators proved to be one of the chief driving forces behind the idea for *Nutmeg*. This is only the beginning of Poppy and Cassia's journey, and while they do fare better than Pauline and Juliet, neither can be expected to make it out of this story unscathed.

END

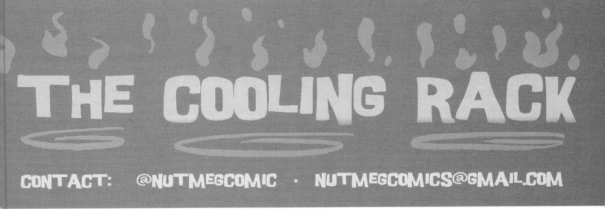

THE COOLING RACK

CONTACT: @NUTMEGCOMIC · NUTMEGCOMICS@GMAIL.COM

Heavenly Creatures
by James F. Wright

"'Tis indeed a miracle, one must feel, /
That two such heavenly creatures are real."

Let's talk about Peter Jackson's *Heavenly Creatures* for a moment. And by "let's talk," I mean, "let me talk at you." Whether we acknowledge it or not, the things we watch and read and listen to, as much as the things we experience ourselves, influence the stories we tell. The comic you hold in your hands (or, possibly, on your digital comics device) has had a wealth of various media and experiences as its inspirations—*Mean Girls, Veronica Mars, Nancy Drew, Breaking Bad, Betty & Veronica,* etc.—but for me, none looms larger than *Heavenly Creatures.* I first saw the film, which was released in 1994, as a sophomore in college back in 2000, but it's one that has stuck with me in a way few others have. It also marks Peter Jackson's first post-splatstick/gross-out film, coming in the wake of Bad Taste, *Meet the Feebles* and *Dead Alive* (or *Braindead* if you're outside the U.S.) If you haven't seen *Heavenly Creatures,* I do highly recommend it and it's one of my ten favorite films, though I hasten to add that it is **most definitely an R-rated film** and a bit traumatic.)

Heavenly Creatures, based on actual events, tells the story of Pauline and Juliet, a pair of teenaged girls growing up in the mid-1950s in New Zealand who form a fast friendship and a nearly unbreakable bond. The two discover each other when Juliet moves to Christchurch from England with her family and, attending Pauline's school, proves herself to be a free spirit and a breath of fresh air to the more aloof Pauline. They connect over a love of Mario Lanza ("The world's greatest tenor."), a hatred of Orson Welles ("The most hideous man alive.") and their mutual scars—Pauline's on her leg from osteomyelitis, Juliet's on her lungs ("All the best people have bad chests and bone diseases.") What's more, they build an elaborate fantasy world, the Kingdom of Borovnia, which comes to life not only in their detailed recounts of imagined court intrigues and conquests, but also in the clay models they construct of the kingdom's sovereigns and subjects.

As one might expect from teenagers, their parents and the adults in their orbit don't understand them. However, added into this is the time period and conservative environment where they find themselves, and a friendship this strong—especially one bordering on love—between two girls is considered a scandalous thing. Faced with what they see as an inevitable decision, Pauline's parents make preparations to separate their daughter from the all-consuming influence of Juliet. And it's here where the darknes lurking in the wings of the film takes center stage, as the two girls plot to kill Pauline's mother.

Bryan Seaton - Publisher • Kevin Freeman - President • Dave Dwonch - Creative Director • Shawn Gabborin - Editor In Chief
Jamal Igle & Kelly Dale- Co-Directors of Marketing • Social Media Director - Jim Dietz • Education Outreach Director - Jeremy Whit
Chad Cicconi - ate all the brownies • Colleen Boyd - Associate Editor

NUTMEG #2, April 2015. Copyright Jackie Crofts and James F. Wright, 2015. Published by Action Lab Comics. All rights reserved. All characters are fictional. Any likeness to anyone livi
dead is purely coincidental. No part of this publication may be reproduced or transmitted without permission, except for small excerpts for review purposes. First Printing. Printed in Ca

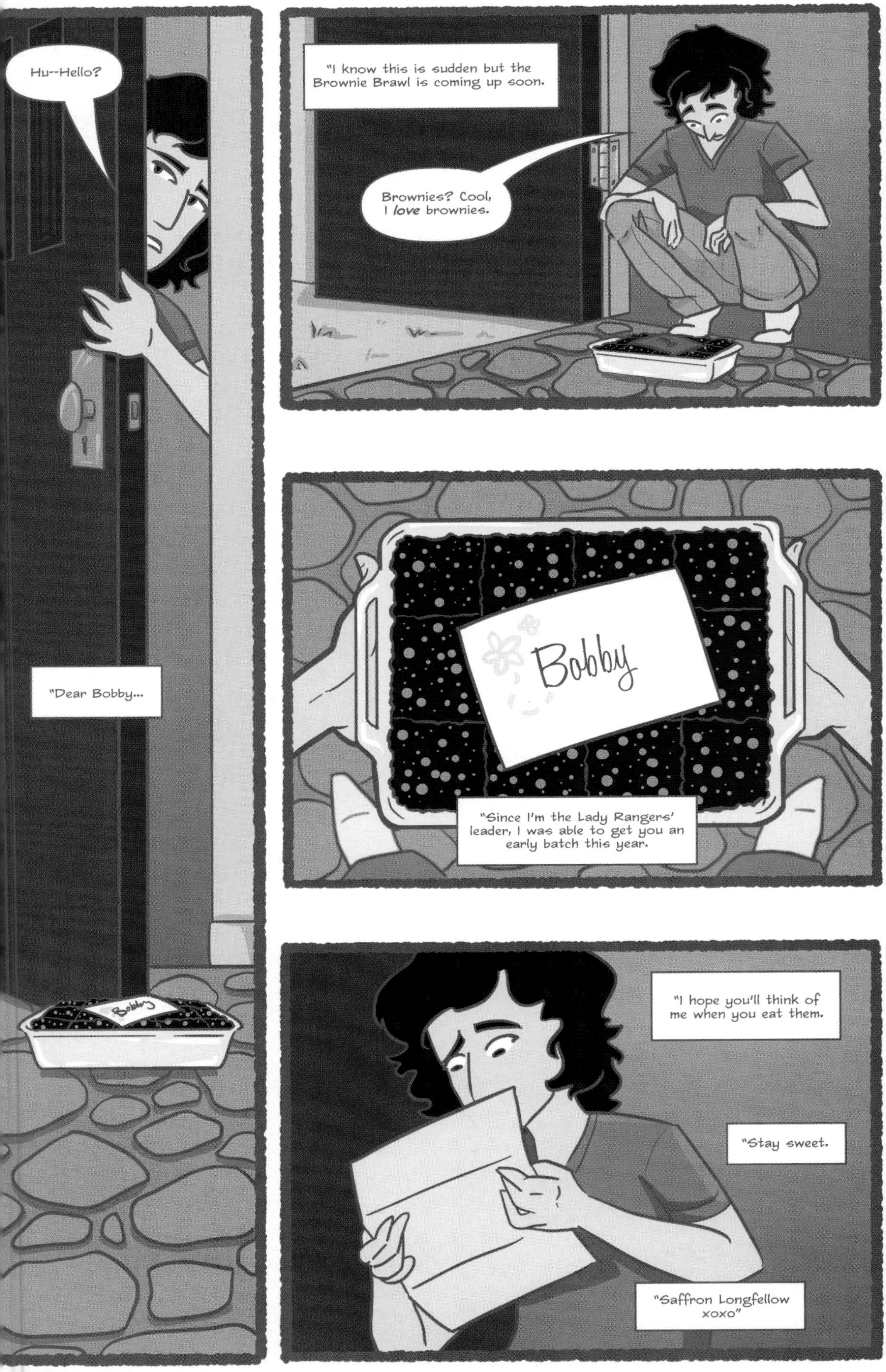
Hu--Hello?
"Dear Bobby...
"I know this is sudden but the Brownie Brawl is coming up soon.
Brownies? Cool, I *love* brownies.
Bobby
"Since I'm the Lady Rangers' leader, I was able to get you an early batch this year.
"I hope you'll think of me when you eat them.
"Stay sweet.
"Saffron Longfellow xoxo"

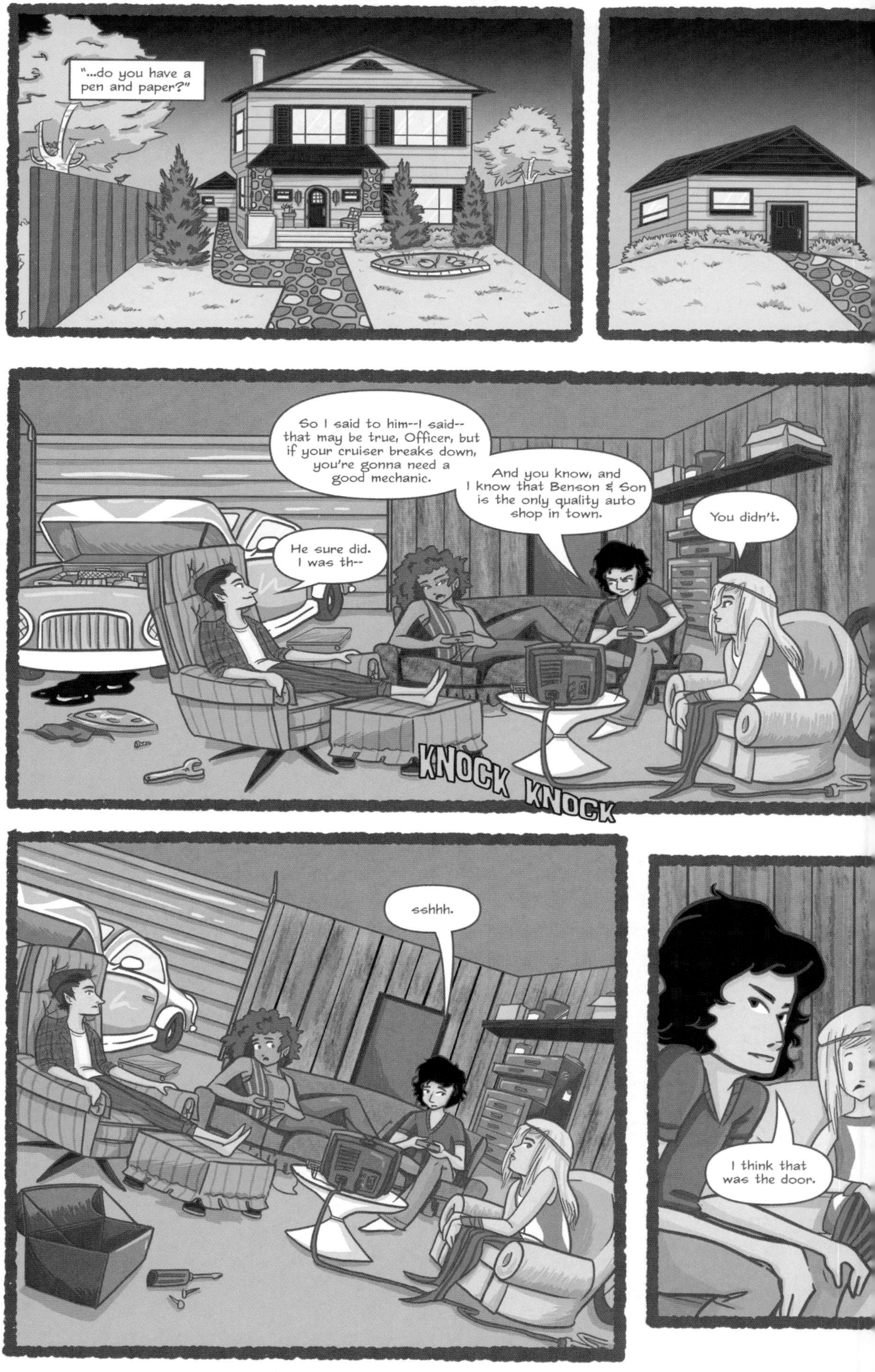
"...do you have a pen and paper?"
So I said to him--I said--that may be true, Officer, but if your cruiser breaks down, you're gonna need a good mechanic.
He sure did. I was th--
And you know, and I know that Benson & Son is the only quality auto shop in town.
You didn't.
KNOCK KNOCK
sshhh.
I think that was the door.

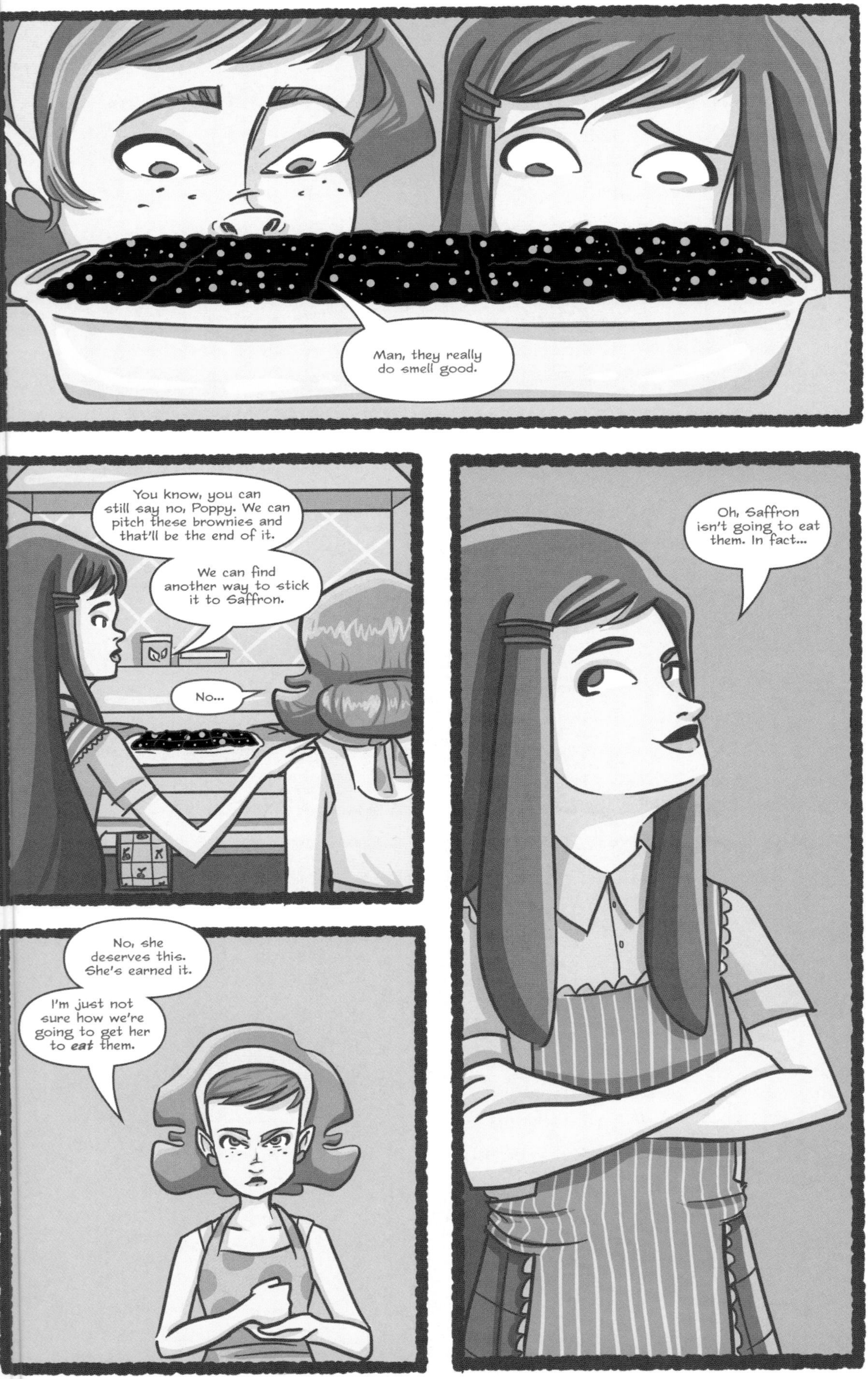
Man, they really do smell good.
You know, you can still say no, Poppy. We can pitch these brownies and that'll be the end of it.
We can find another way to stick it to Saffron.
No...
Oh, Saffron isn't going to eat them. In fact...
No, she deserves this. She's earned it.
I'm just not sure how we're going to get her to *eat* them.

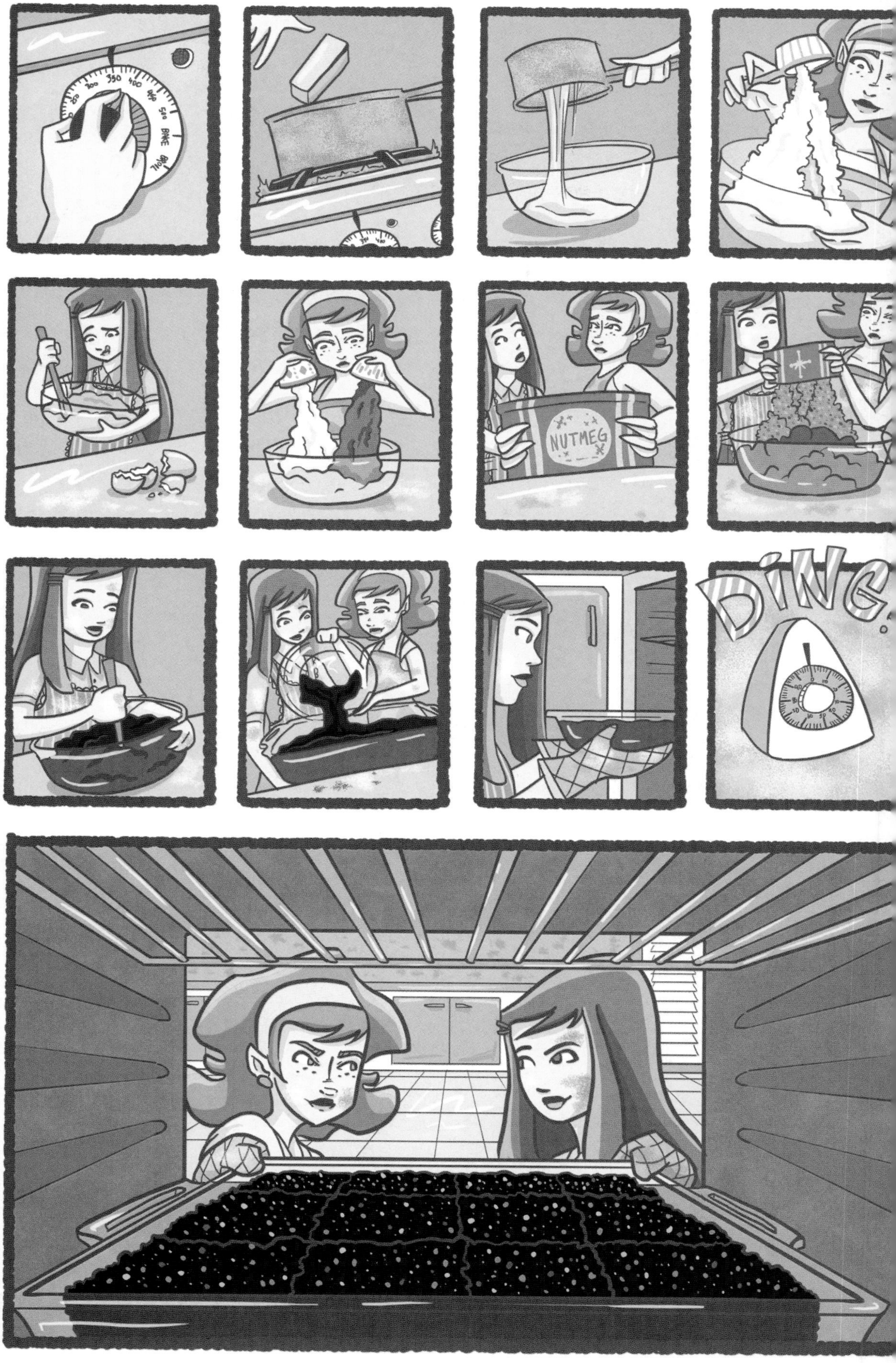
BAKE
BROIL
NUTMEG
DING

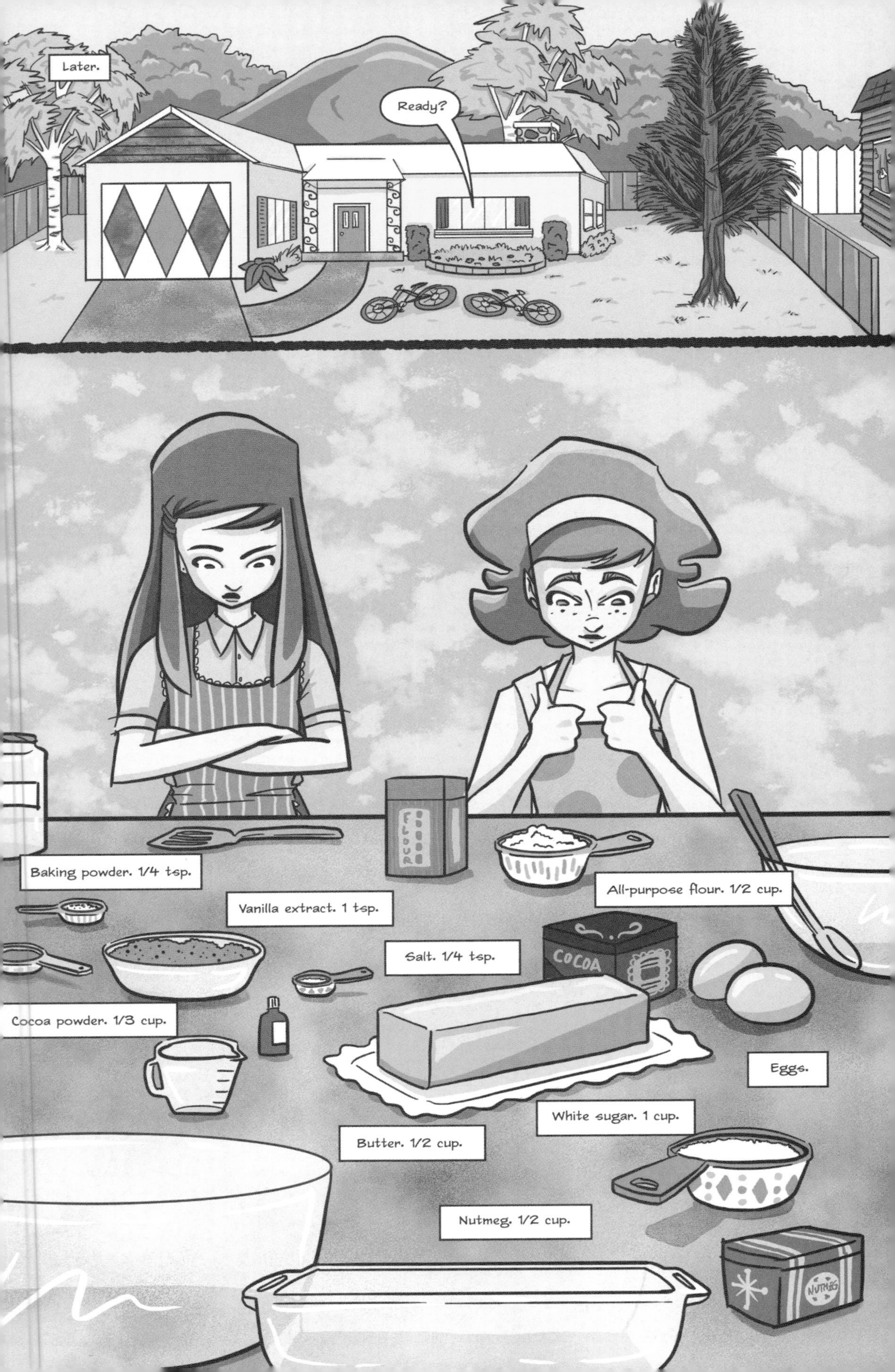
Later.
Ready?
Baking powder. 1/4 tsp.
Vanilla extract. 1 tsp.
All-purpose flour. 1/2 cup.
Salt. 1/4 tsp.
Cocoa powder. 1/3 cup.
Eggs.
White sugar. 1 cup.
Butter. 1/2 cup.
Nutmeg. 1/2 cup.
FLOUR
COCOA
NUTMEG

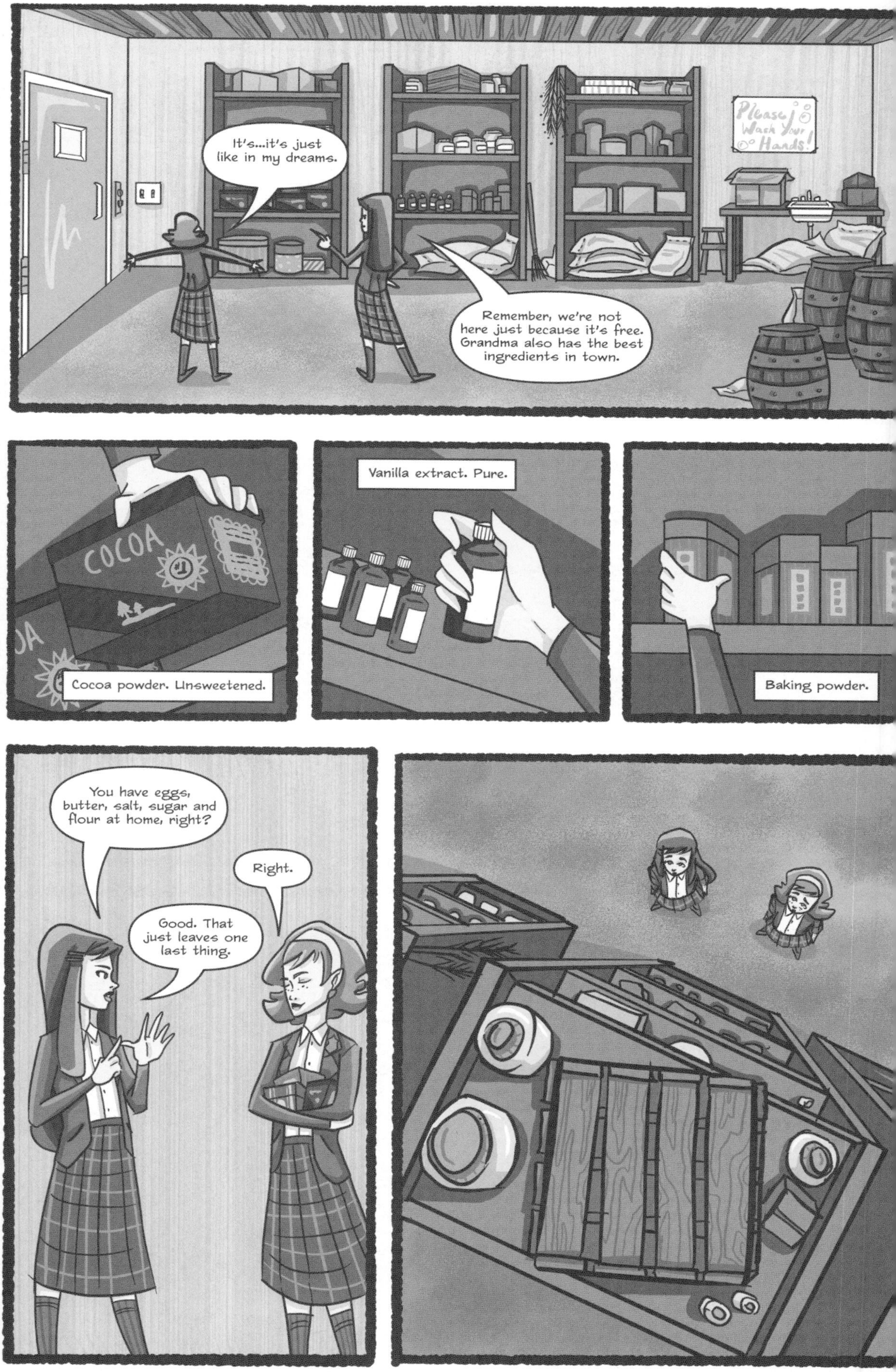
It's...it's just like in my dreams.
Remember, we're not here just because it's free. Grandma also has the best ingredients in town.
Please Wash Your Hands!
COCOA
Cocoa powder. Unsweetened.
Vanilla extract. Pure.
Baking powder.
You have eggs, butter, salt, sugar and flour at home, right?
Right.
Good. That just leaves one last thing.

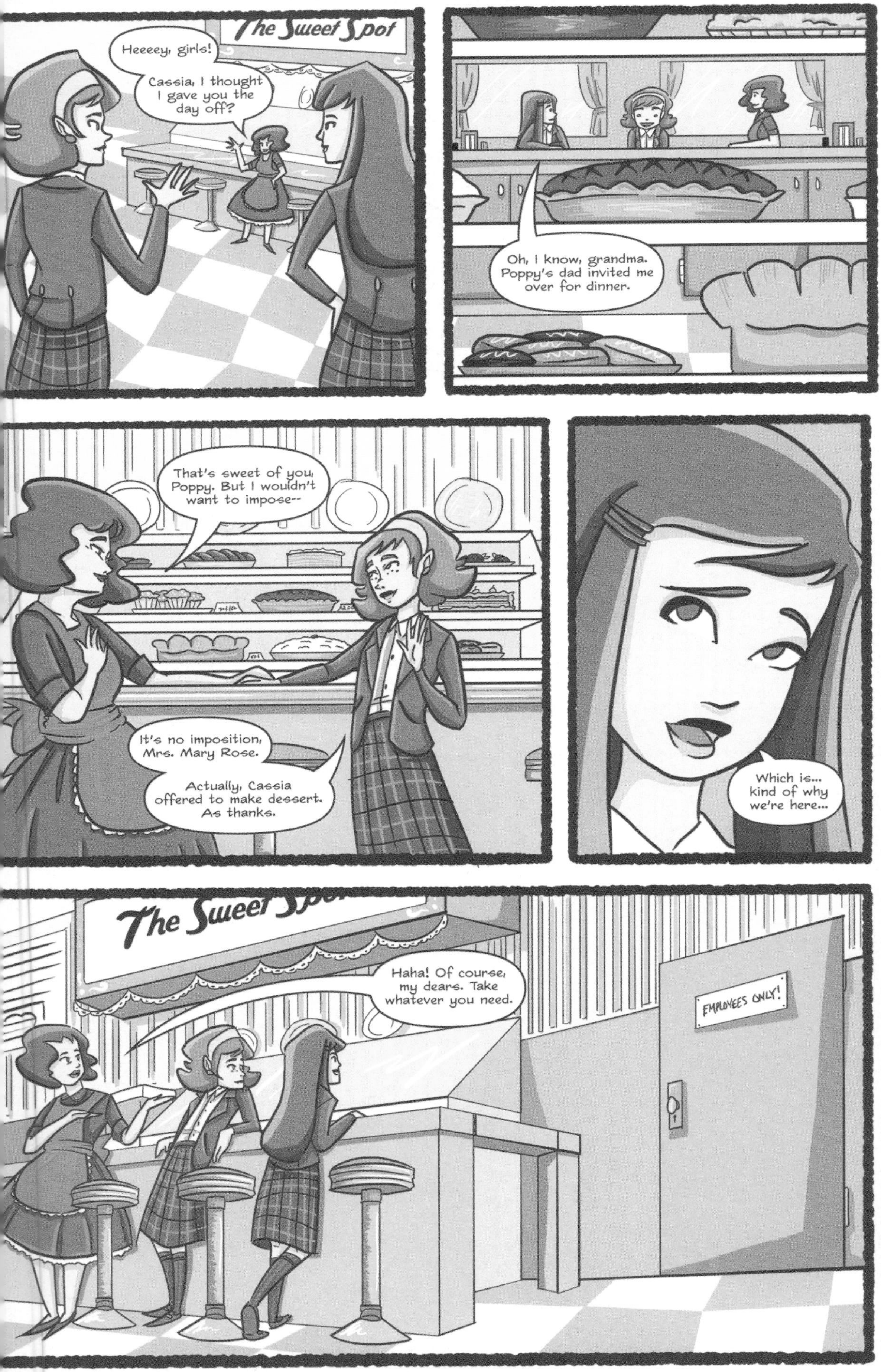
The Sweet Spot
Heeeey, girls!
Cassia, I thought I gave you the day off?
Oh, I know, grandma. Poppy's dad invited me over for dinner.
That's sweet of you, Poppy. But I wouldn't want to impose--
It's no imposition, Mrs. Mary Rose.
Actually, Cassia offered to make dessert. As thanks.
Which is... kind of why we're here...
The Sweet Spot
Haha! Of course, my dears. Take whatever you need.
EMPLOYEES ONLY!

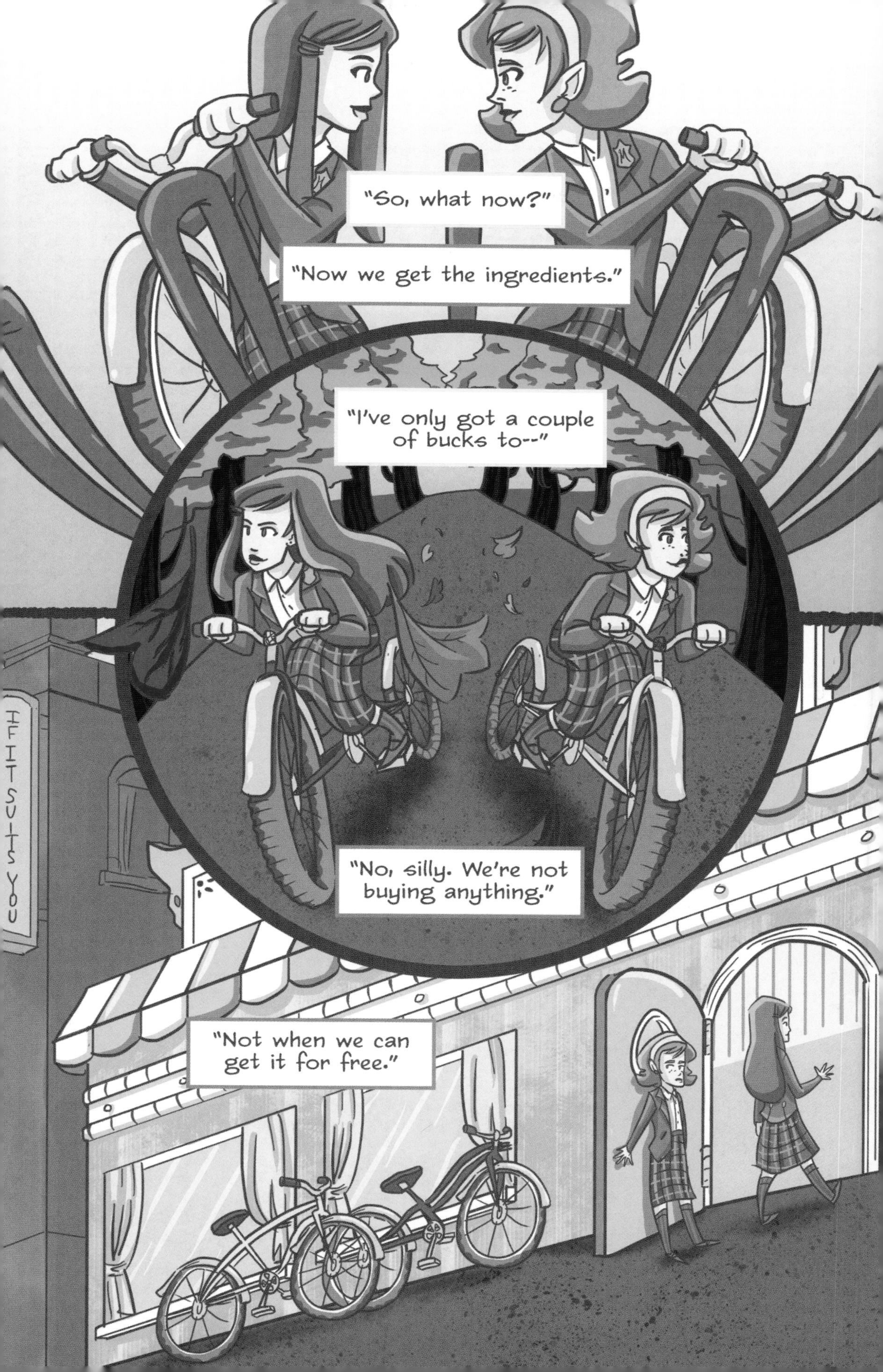
"So, what now?"
"Now we get the ingredients."
"I've only got a couple of bucks to--"
"No, silly. We're not buying anything."
IF IT SUITS YOU
"Not when we can get it for free."

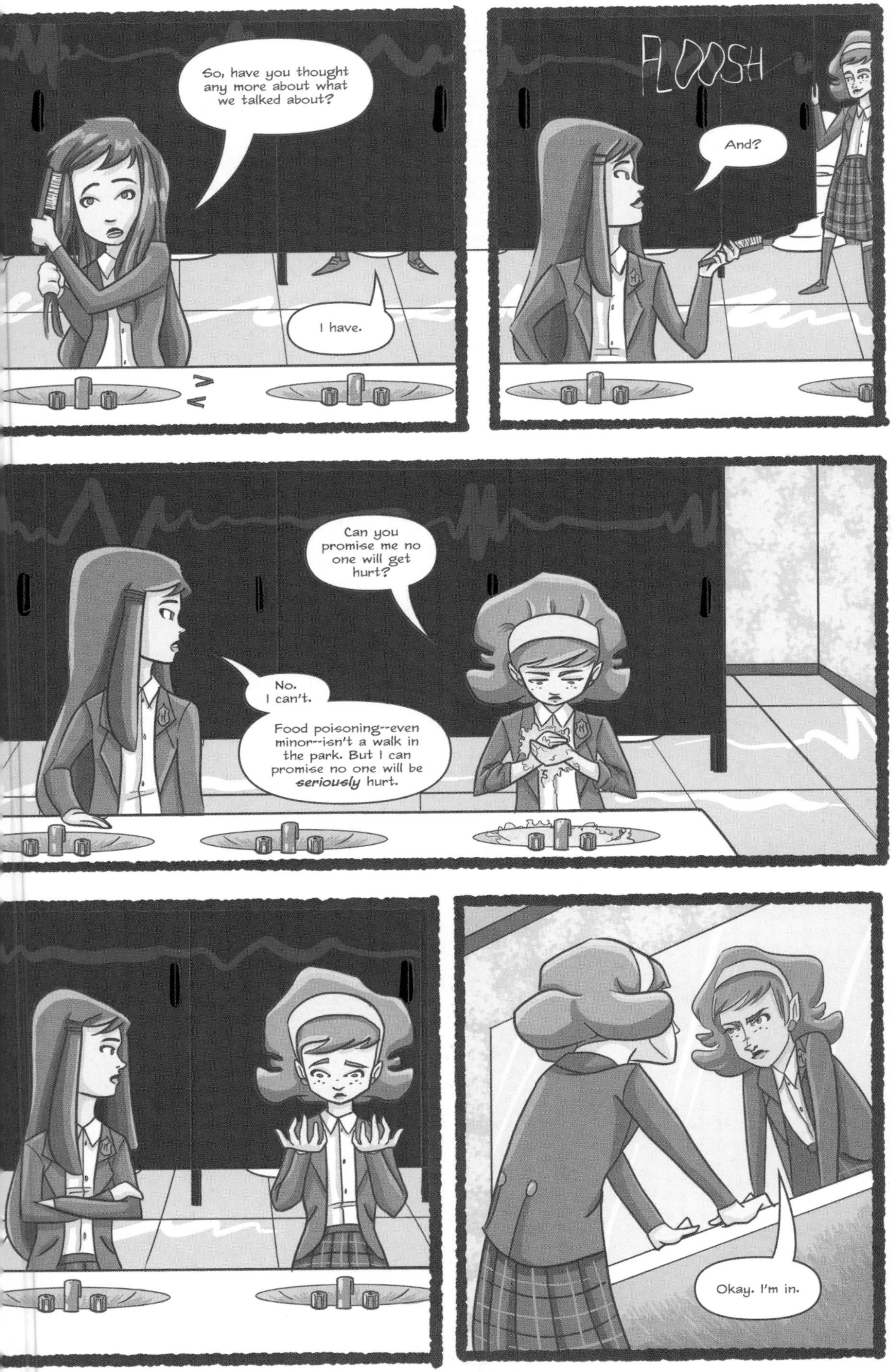
So, have you thought any more about what we talked about?
I have.
FLOOSH
And?
Can you promise me no one will get hurt?
No. I can't.
Food poisoning--even minor--isn't a walk in the park. But I can promise no one will be *seriously* hurt.
Okay. I'm in.

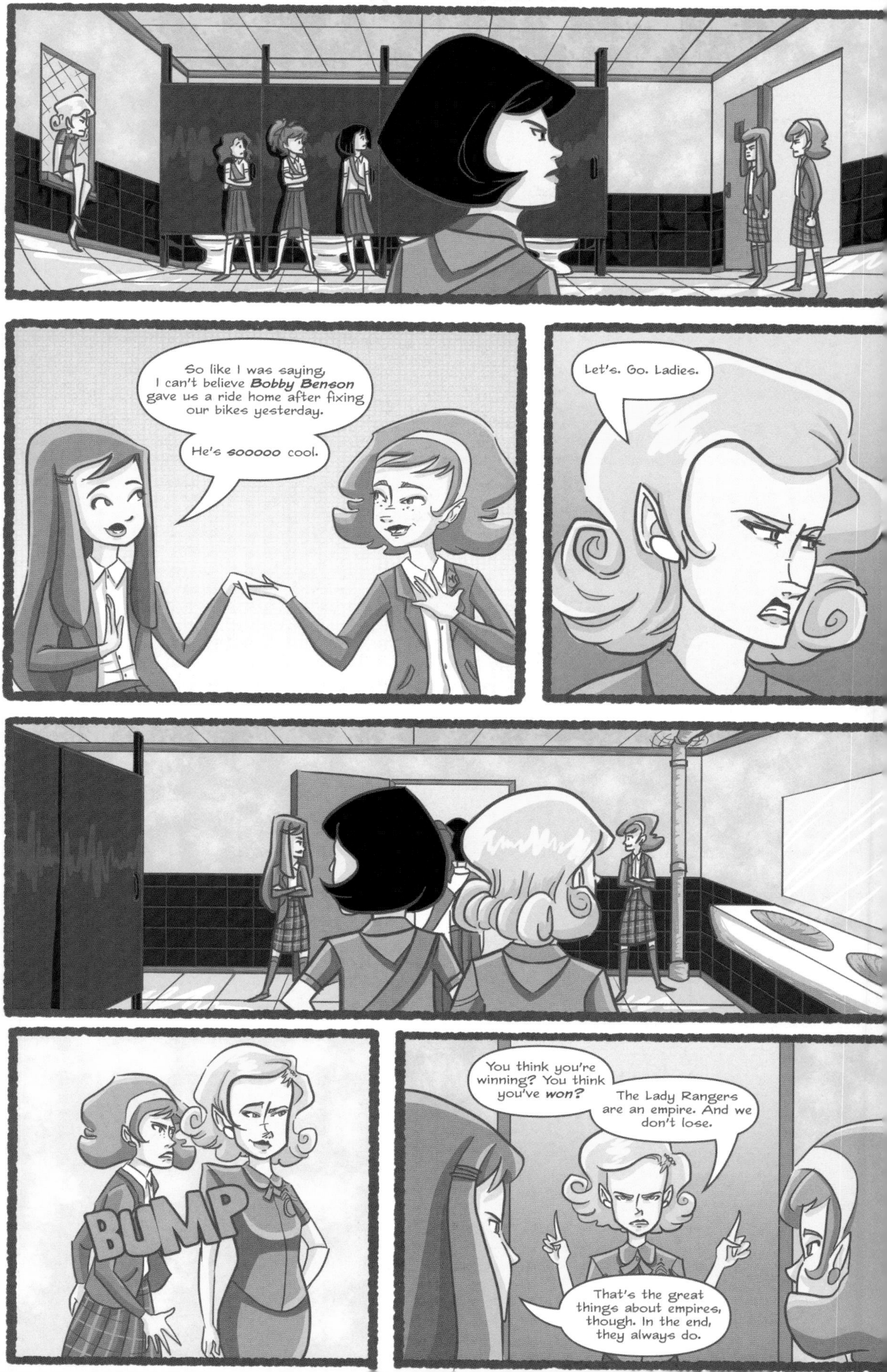
So like I was saying, I can't believe ***Bobby Benson*** gave us a ride home after fixing our bikes yesterday.
He's ***sooooo*** cool.
Let's. Go. Ladies.
BUMP
You think you're winning? You think you've ***won?***
The Lady Rangers are an empire. And we don't lose.
That's the great things about empires, though. In the end, they always do.

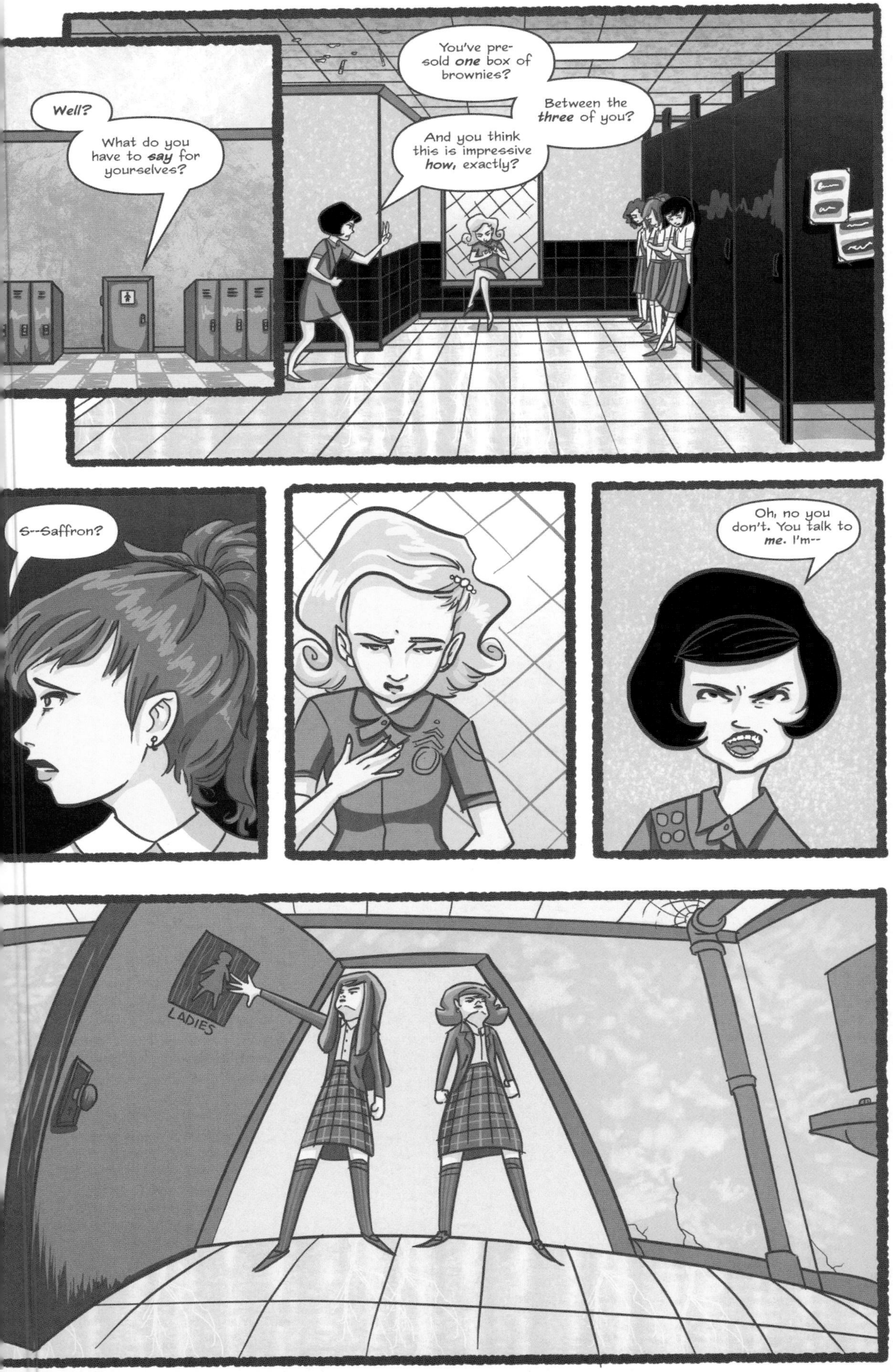
Well?
What do you have to say for yourselves?
You've pre-sold one box of brownies?
Between the three of you?
And you think this is impressive how, exactly?
S--Saffron?
Oh, no you don't. You talk to me. I'm--
LADIES

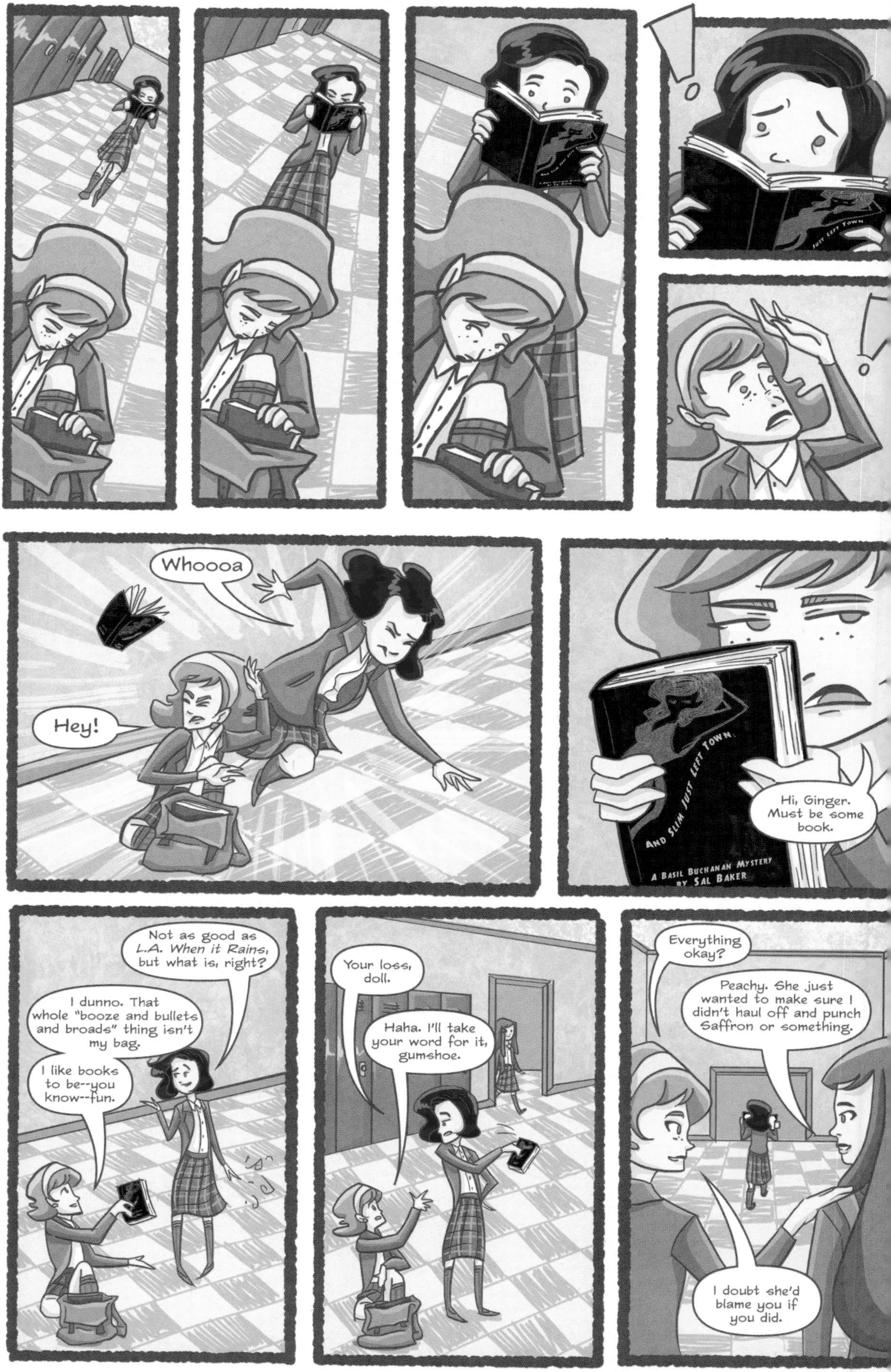
Just Left Town
Whoooa
Hey!
And Slim Just Left Town
A Basil Buchanan Mystery by Sal Baker
Hi, Ginger. Must be some book.
Not as good as *L.A. When it Rains*, but what is, right?
I dunno. That whole "booze and bullets and broads" thing isn't my bag.
I like books to be--you know--fun.
Your loss, doll.
Haha. I'll take your word for it, gumshoe.
Everything okay?
Peachy. She just wanted to make sure I didn't haul off and punch Saffron or something.
I doubt she'd blame you if you did.

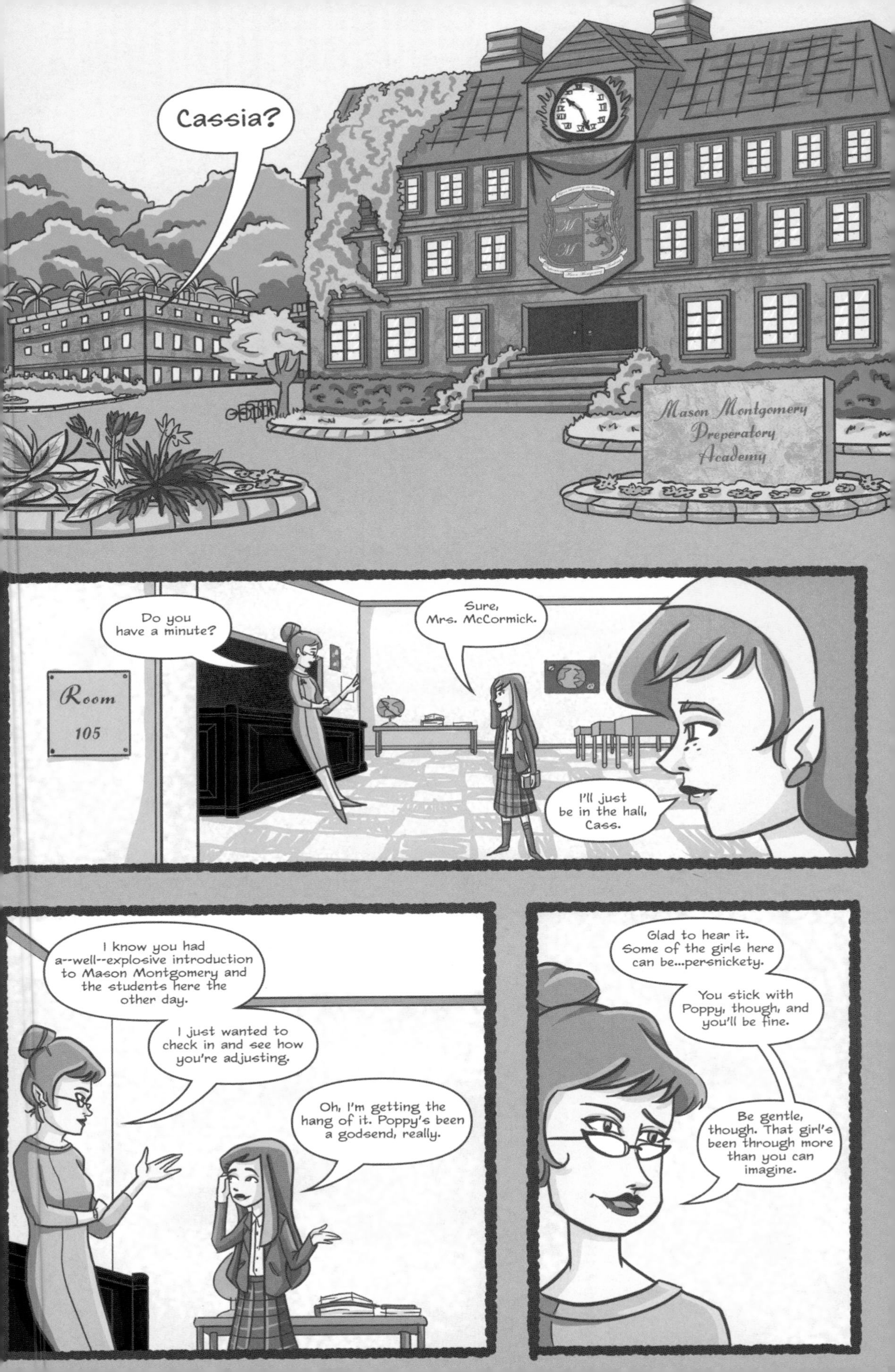

Cassia?
Mason Montgomery Dreperatory Academy
Do you have a minute?
Sure, Mrs. McCormick.
Room 105
I'll just be in the hall, Cass.
I know you had a--well--explosive introduction to Mason Montgomery and the students here the other day.
I just wanted to check in and see how you're adjusting.
Oh, I'm getting the hang of it. Poppy's been a godsend, really.
Glad to hear it. Some of the girls here can be...persnickety.
You stick with Poppy, though, and you'll be fine.
Be gentle, though. That girl's been through more than you can imagine.

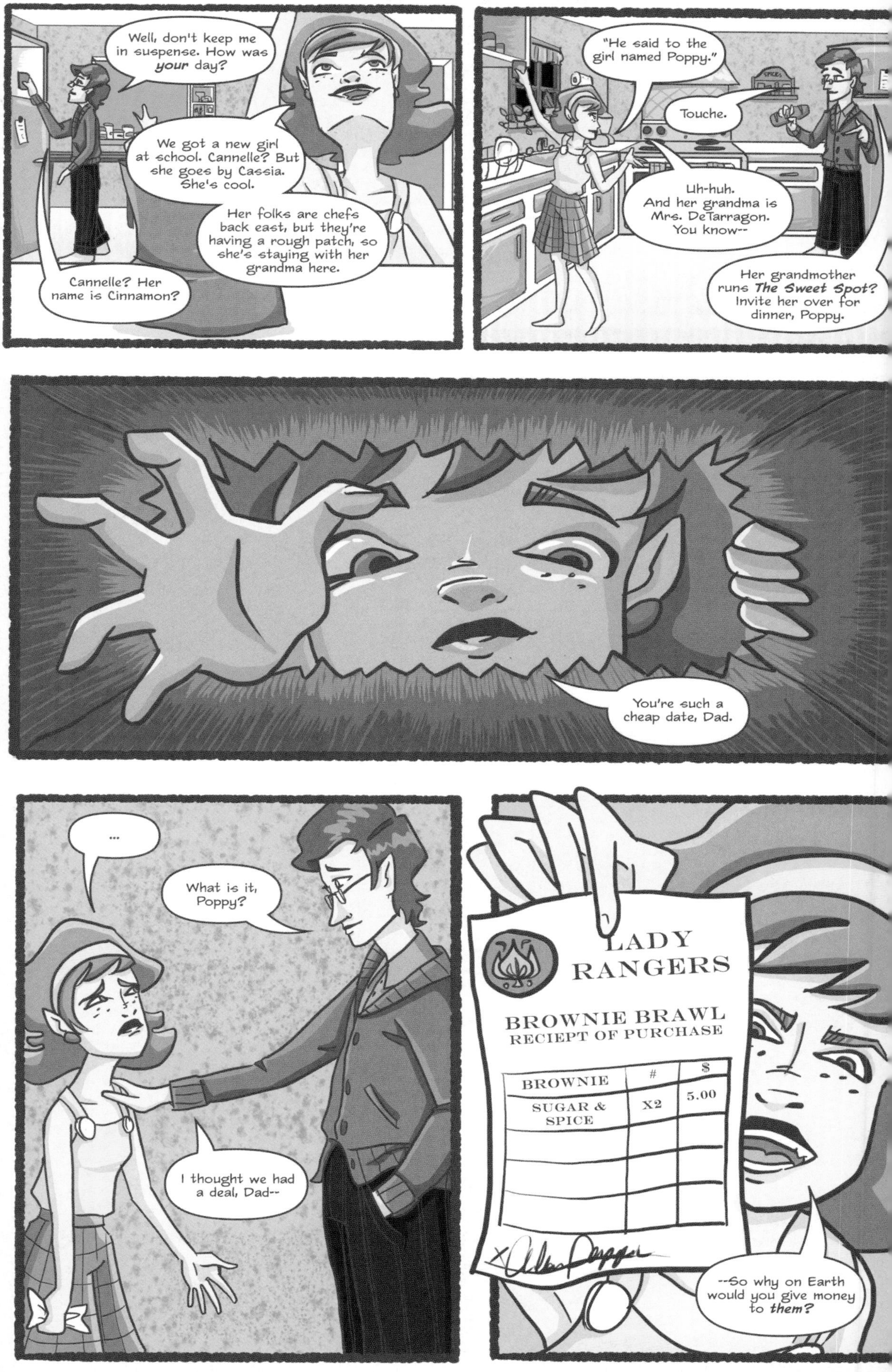
Well, don't keep me in suspense. How was *your* day?
We got a new girl at school. Cannelle? But she goes by Cassia. She's cool.
Her folks are chefs back east, but they're having a rough patch, so she's staying with her grandma here.
Cannelle? Her name is Cinnamon?
"He said to the girl named Poppy."
Touche.
Uh-huh. And her grandma is Mrs. DeTarragon. You know--
Her grandmother runs *The Sweet Spot*? Invite her over for dinner, Poppy.
You're such a cheap date, Dad.
...
What is it, Poppy?
I thought we had a deal, Dad--
LADY RANGERS
BROWNIE BRAWL
RECIEPT OF PURCHASE
BROWNIE
#
$
SUGAR & SPICE
X2
5.00
--So why on Earth would you give money to *them*?

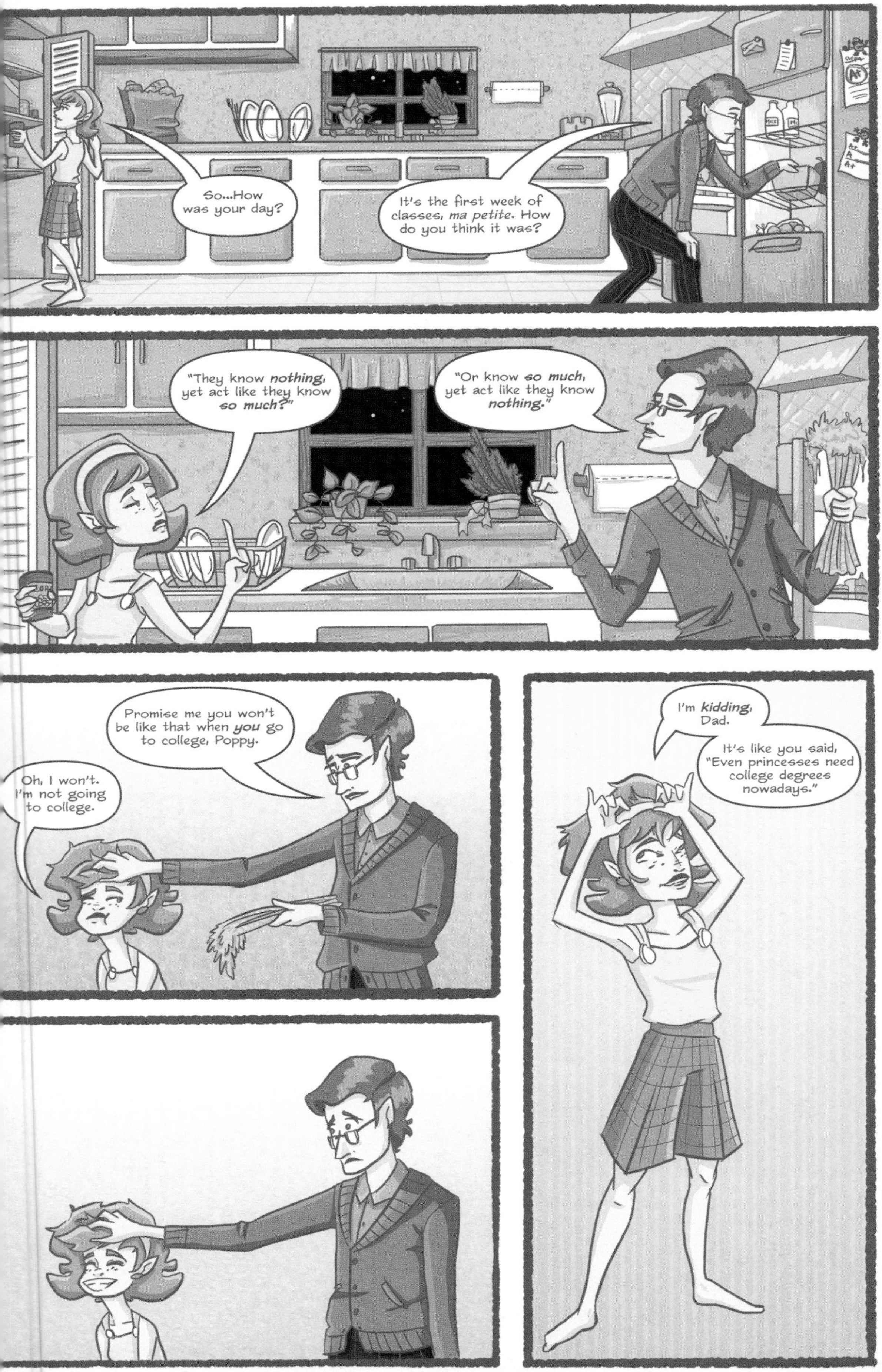
So...How was your day?
It's the first week of classes, *ma petite*. How do you think it was?
"They know **nothing**, yet act like they know **so much**?"
"Or know **so much**, yet act like they know **nothing**."
Promise me you won't be like that when **you** go to college, Poppy.
Oh, I won't. I'm not going to college.
I'm **kidding**, Dad.
It's like you said, "Even princesses need college degrees nowadays."

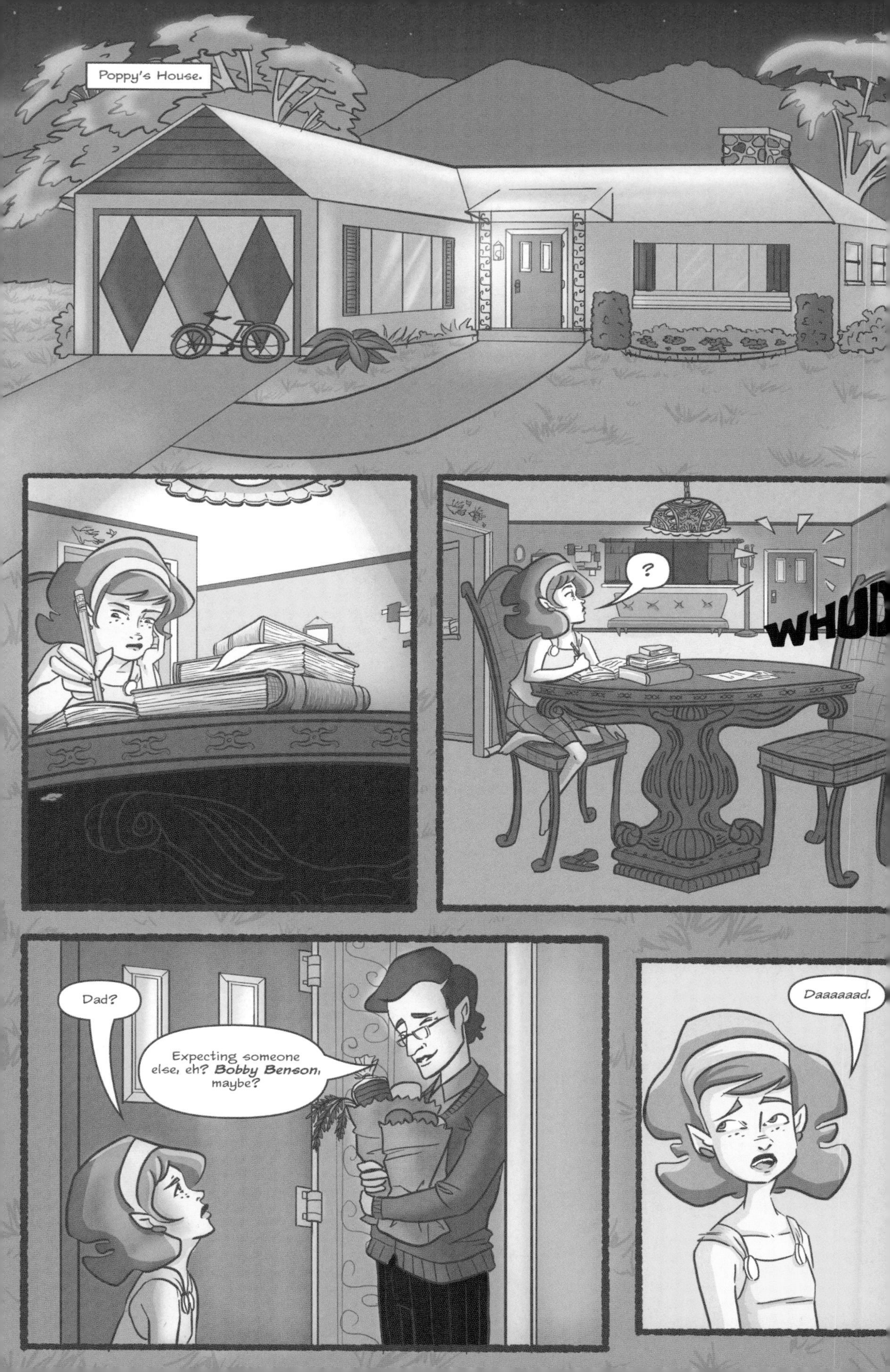
Poppy's House.
?
WHUD
Dad?
Expecting someone else, eh? Bobby Benson, maybe?
Daaaaaad.

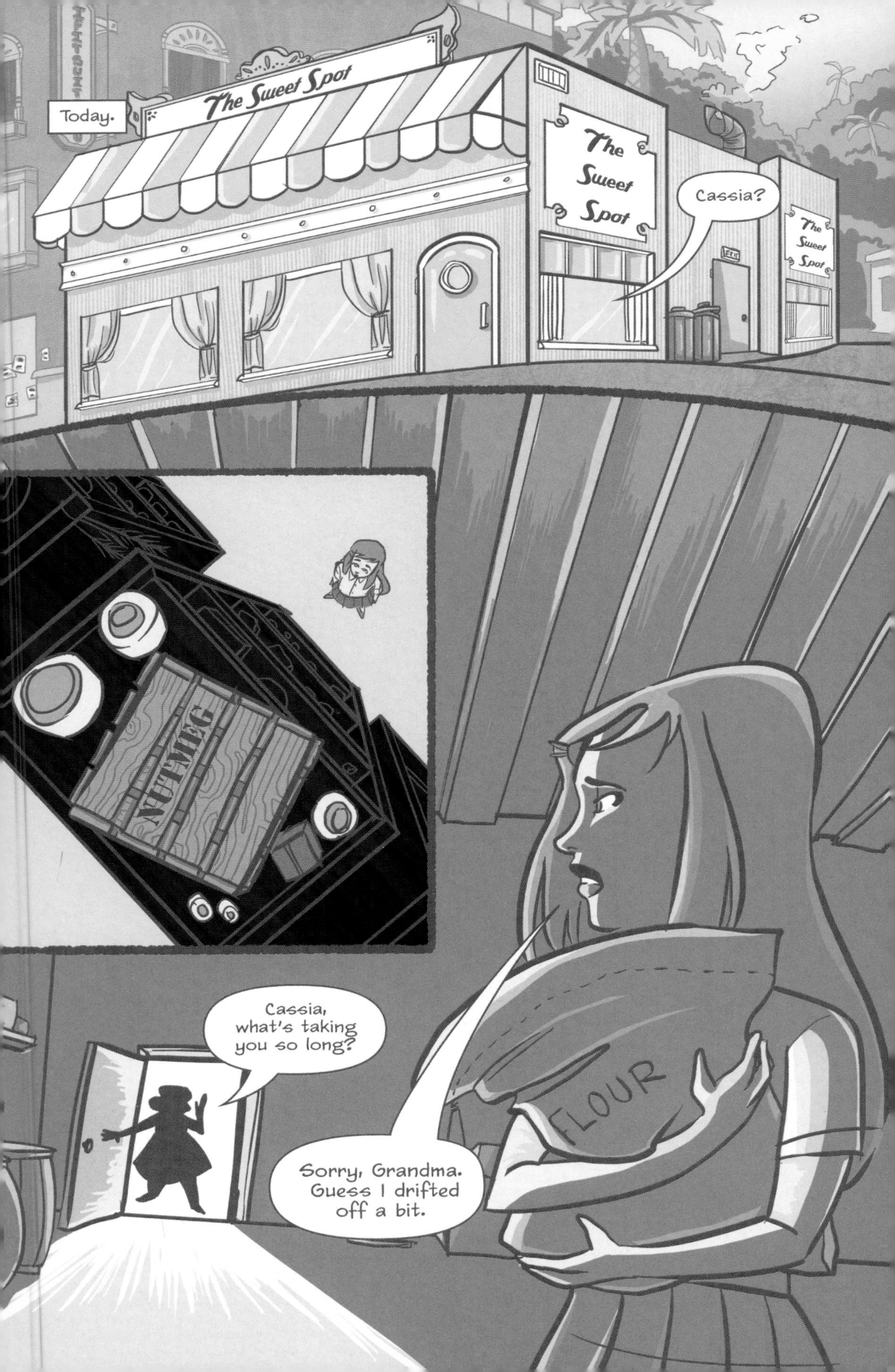
Today.
The Sweet Spot
The Sweet Spot
The Sweet Spot
Cassia?
NUTMEG
Cassia, what's taking you so long?
FLOUR
Sorry, Grandma. Guess I drifted off a bit.

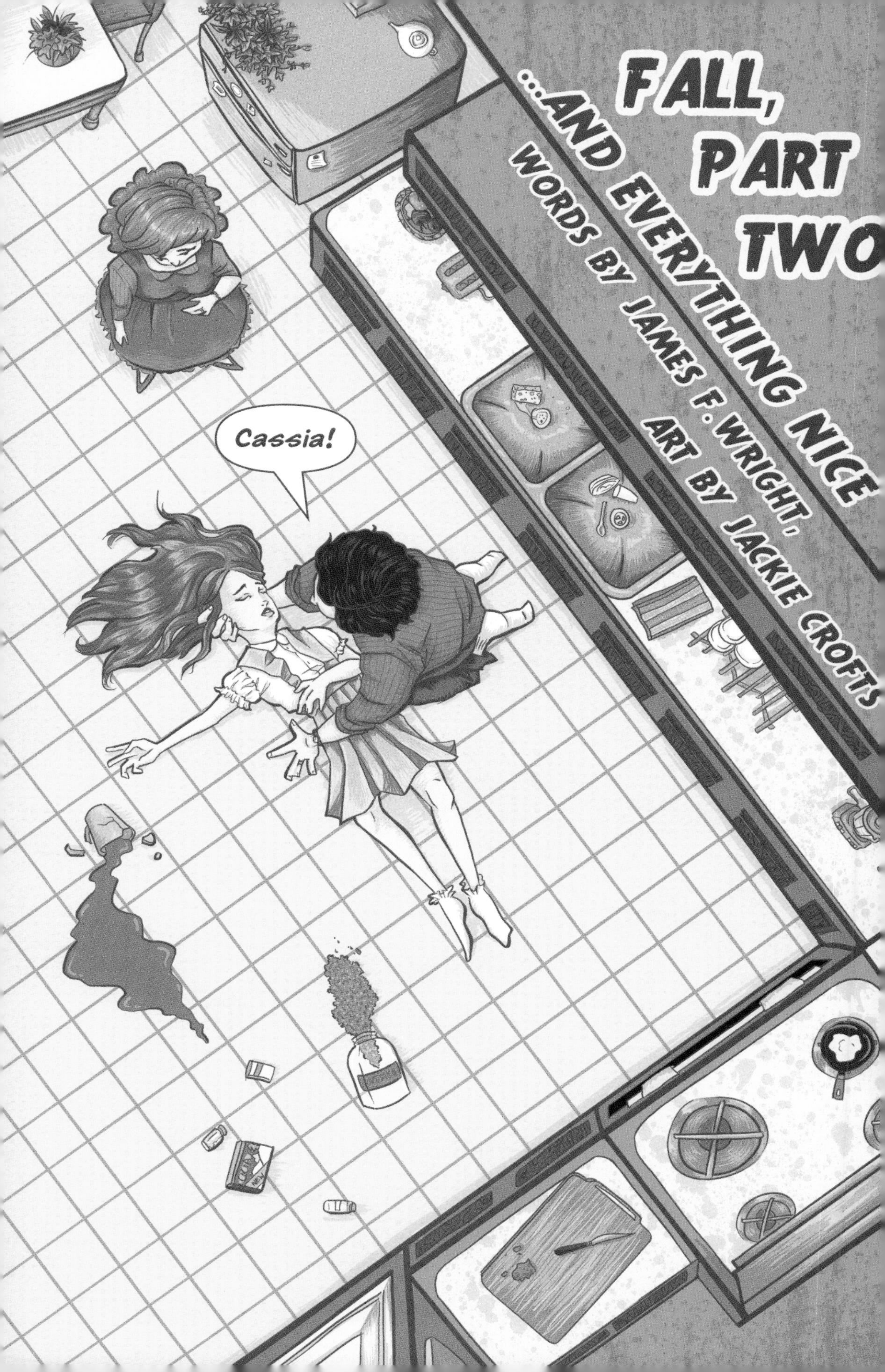

FALL, PART TWO
...AND EVERYTHING NICE
WORDS BY JAMES F. WRIGHT,
ART BY JACKIE CROFTS
Cassia!

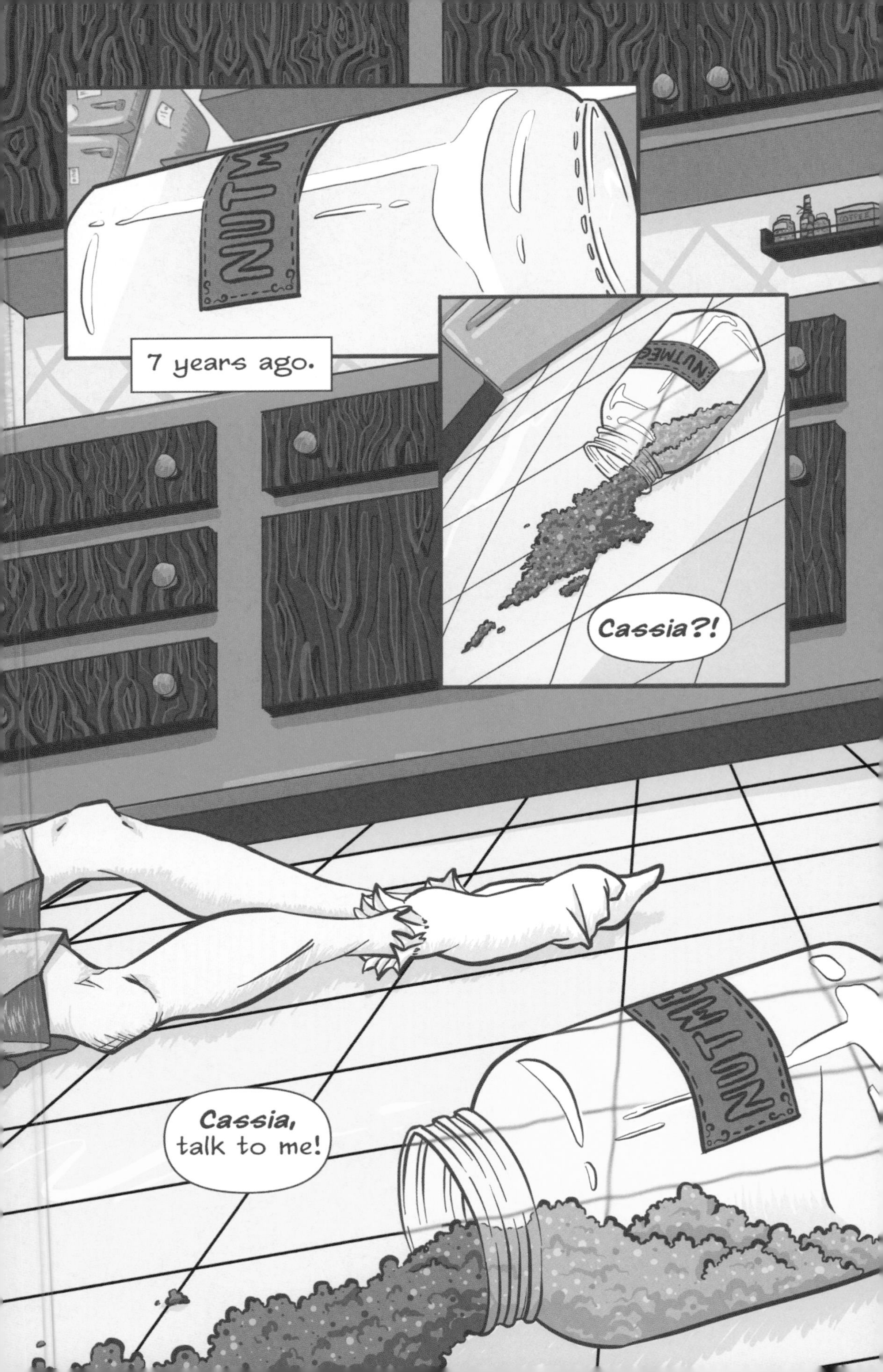
NUTM
7 years ago.
NUTMEG
Cassia?!
NUTMEG
Cassia,
talk to me!

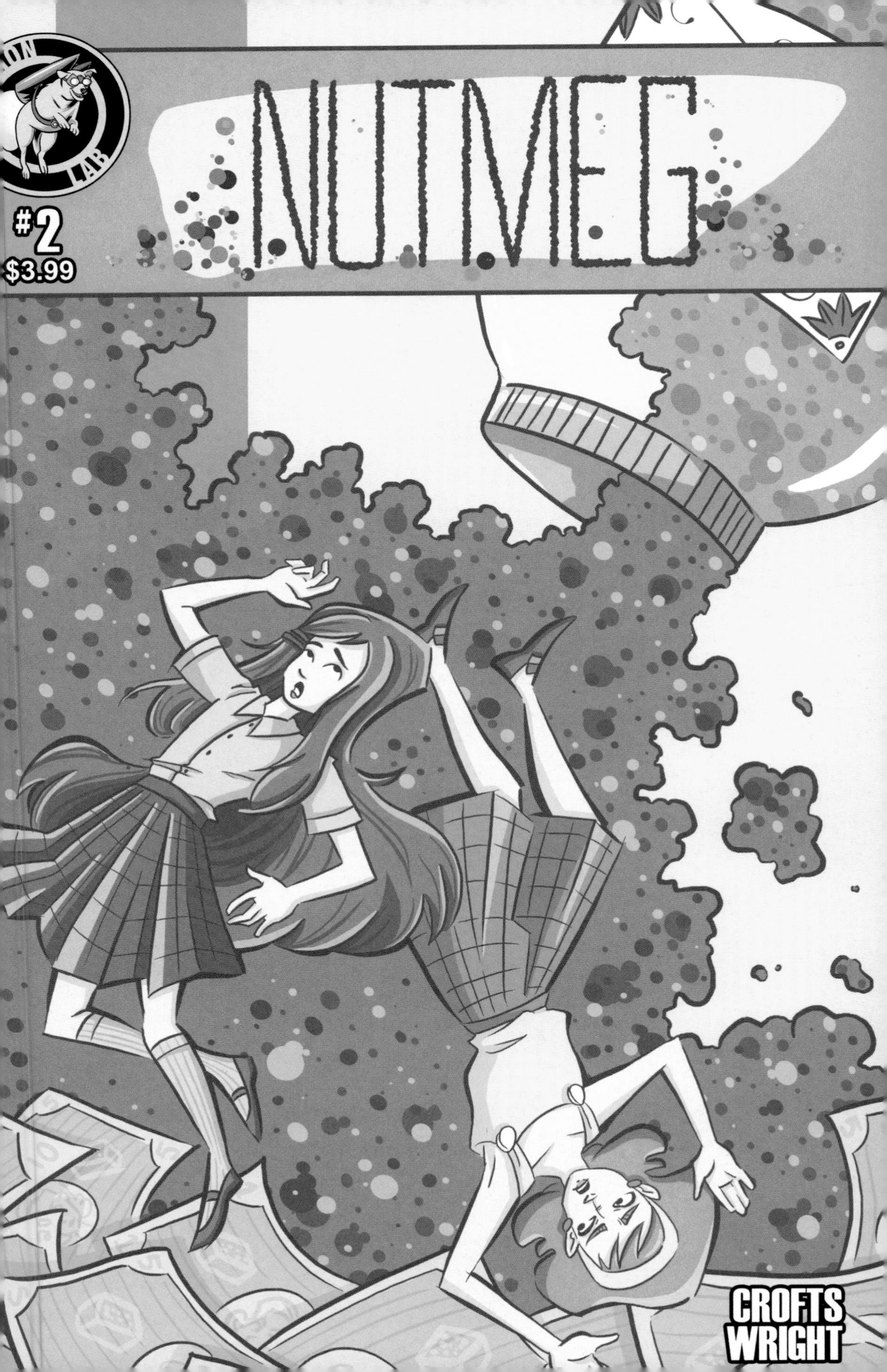
NUTMEG
#2
$3.99
CROFTS
WRIGHT

ACTION LAB

READ MORE NOW

Nutmeg - Action Lab
www.actionlabcomics.com
00111
7 02382 69089 2

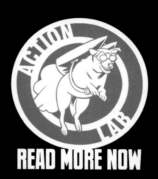

ACTIONLABCOMICS.COM

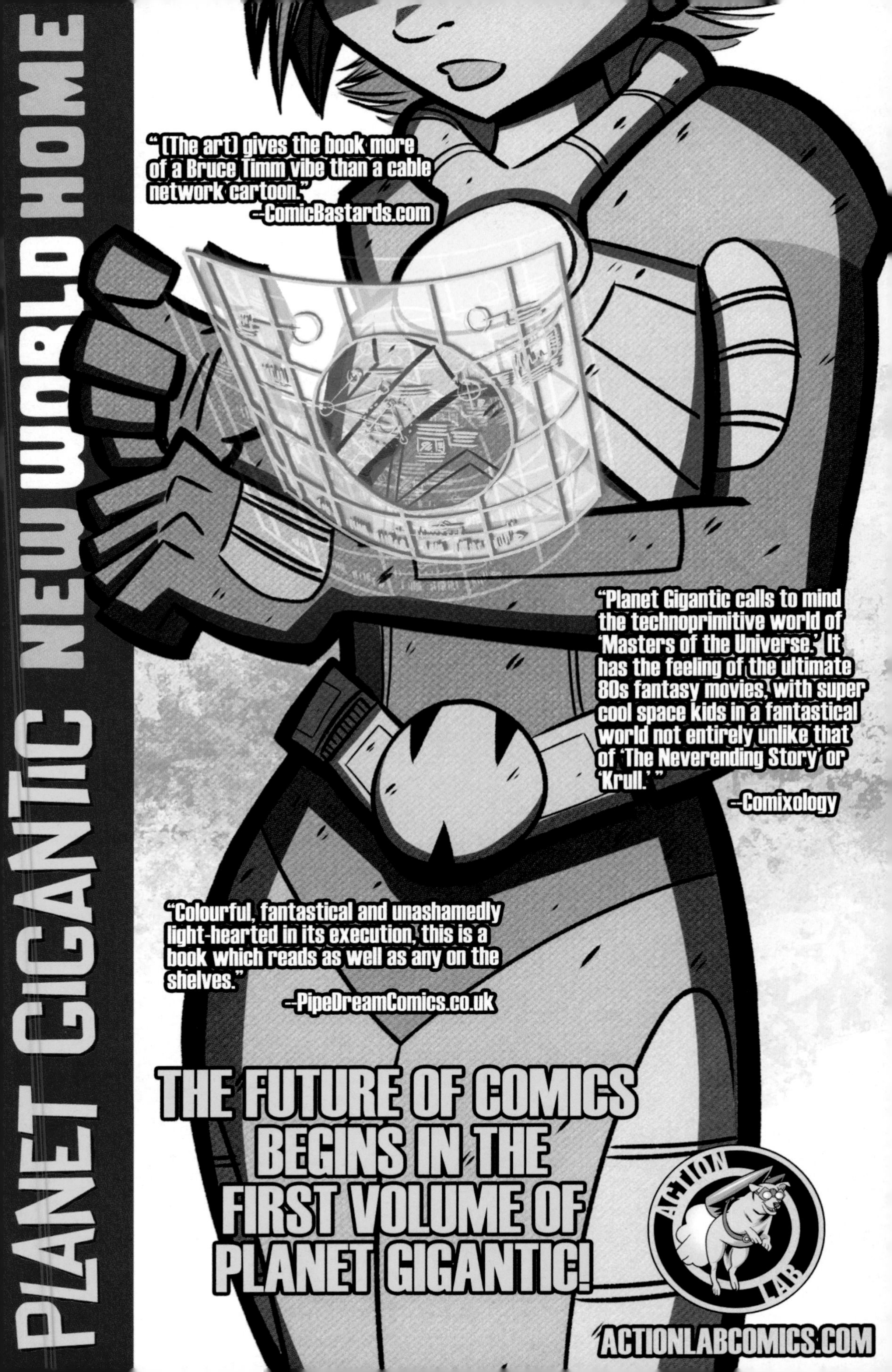
PLANET GIGANTIC NEW WORLD HOME
“[The art] gives the book more of a Bruce Timm vibe than a cable network cartoon.”
--ComicBastards.com
“Planet Gigantic calls to mind the technoprimitive world of ‘Masters of the Universe.’ It has the feeling of the ultimate 80s fantasy movies, with super cool space kids in a fantastical world not entirely unlike that of ‘The Neverending Story’ or ‘Krull.’ ”
--Comixology
“Colourful, fantastical and unashamedly light-hearted in its execution, this is a book which reads as well as any on the shelves.”
--PipeDreamComics.co.uk
THE FUTURE OF COMICS BEGINS IN THE FIRST VOLUME OF PLANET GIGANTIC!
ACTION LAB
ACTIONLABCOMICS.COM

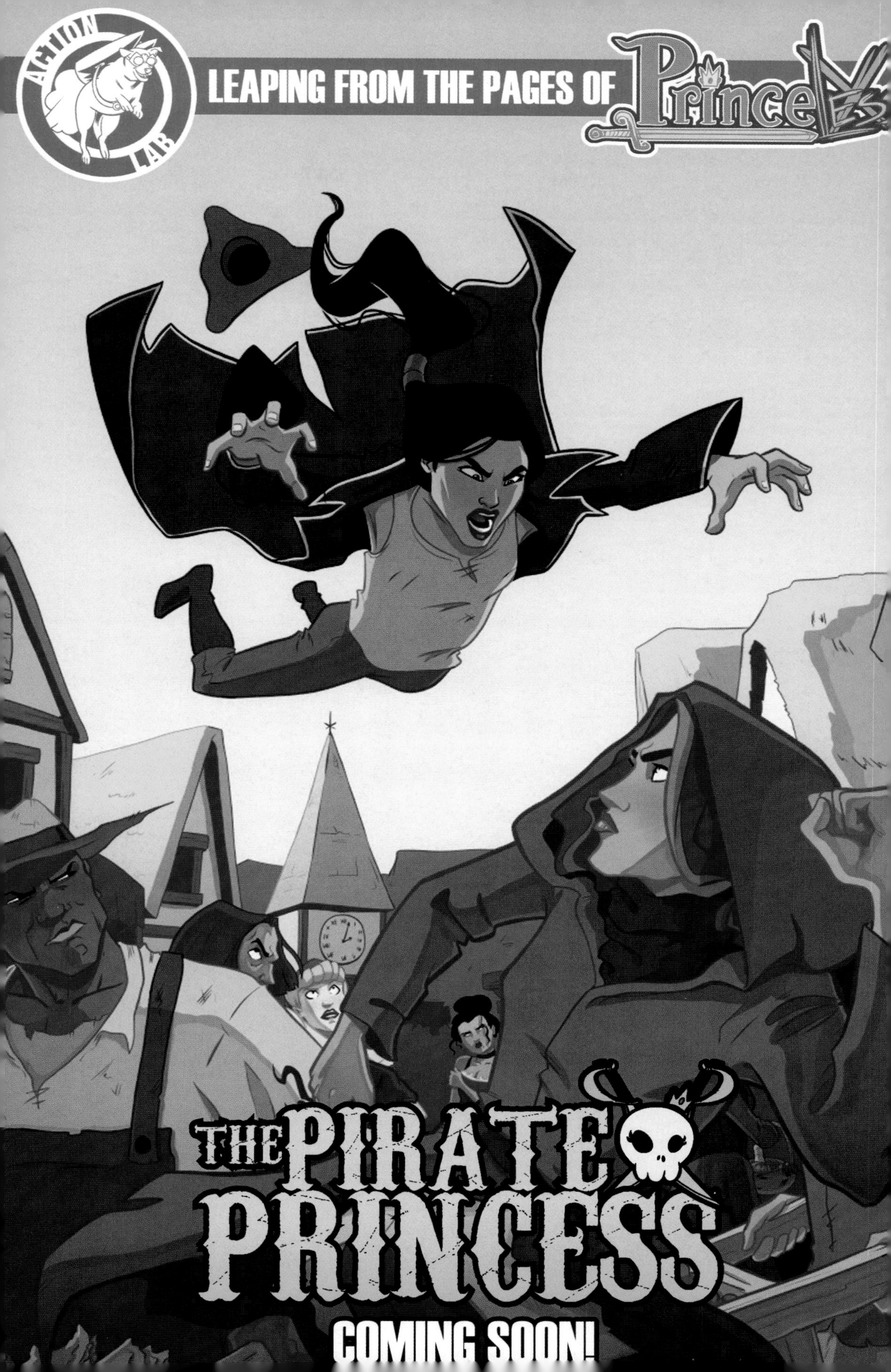
ACTION LAB
LEAPING FROM THE PAGES OF Princeless
THE PIRATE PRINCESS
COMING SOON!

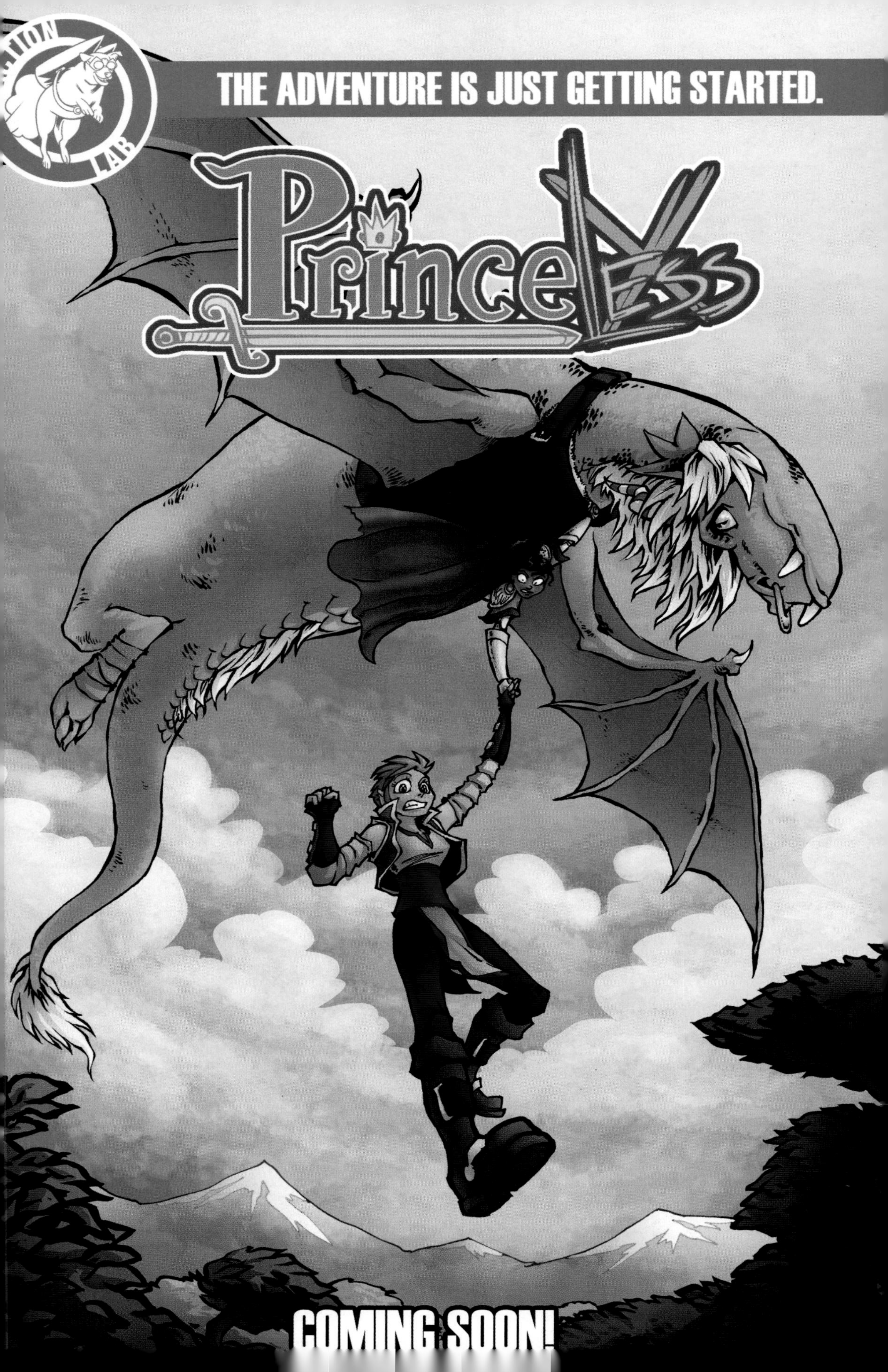

THE ADVENTURE IS JUST GETTING STARTED.
Princeless
COMING SOON!

darkness, but rather examine how their criminal enterprise either changes these special young women, or makes them even more of who they always were. Rest assured that there is a lot in store for everyone here, and that the town of Vista Vale will never be the same.

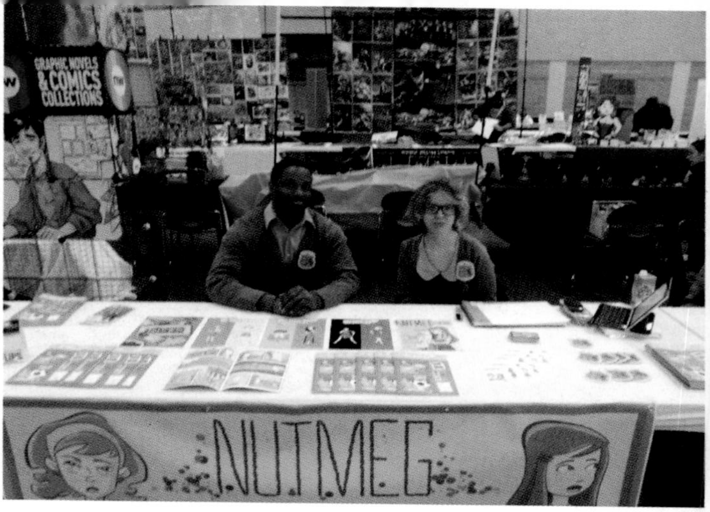
GRAPHIC NOVELS
& COMICS
COLLECTIONS
NUTMEG

And just who the heck are we?

Jackie Crofts is the artist and co-creator of *Nutmeg*. But artist doesn't quite give a full picture of what she does. Anything you see on the page of the book you're holding is all Jackie: line art, colors, even the lettering is her. She is an Indiana native and graduate of IUPUI's School of New Media (Class of 2012) with a focus in game art and game design, and created the mystery game *Stranger Dreams* with Dean Verleger. And she actually uses her degree at her current job, making educational games for Bottom-Line Performance. When she's not making games or comic booking, she spends her time gardening and hanging out with friends. Jackie previously did cover art for an issue of Action Lab's *Princeless* in 2013, though *Nutmeg* represents her first professional foray into comic interiors. Not for nothing, but she's also one of the nicest people you could ever hope to meet.

Jackie would like to thank: My mom and dad for fostering my creativity, and always being accepting of whatever crazy thing I've got going on next. I also want to thank all of my friends, I wouldn't be the person I am today without all the amazing faces I'm surrounded by every day. You make all this hard work worth it and help me through it more than you'll ever know!

James F. Wright is the writer and co-creator of *Nutmeg*. The odds and ends of *Nutmeg* were kicking around in his head since 2011, when his friend Josh Eckert—with whom he co-created *The Geek Zodiac*—suggested he talk to a classmate, Jackie Crofts. After seeing her designs based on the character descriptions he'd sent, it was clear there was no other choice and off they went. James was born in Cleveland, raised in Orlando, graduated from Pitt (Class of 2003), taught in Japan for a while and has lived in Los Angeles since 2007. His laptop and notebooks are littered with scripts, but *Nutmeg* is his second published comics work (after the self-published *Geek Zodiac* Compendium). When he isn't writing comics, he's working in sports TV, quoting *Miller's Crossing* or *Blazing Saddles* and daydreaming about Thai curry, pie, or milkshakes.

James would like to thank: Ma, Pa and Walt for your continued and unfailing love and guidance, and for always supporting my comics reading habit. Penny, because this book is for you and I hope one day you find something in it that speaks to you. And to all of the wonderful, funny, brave and intelligent women in my life. This wouldn't exist without you, and I like to think there's a little bit of all of you in here.

THE COOLING RACK

CONTACT: @NUTMEGCOMIC · NUTMEGCOMICS@GMAIL.COM

Hi, there!

First, we just want to say thank you so much for taking a chance on our book. *Nutmeg* really is a labor of love—a burgeoning teen girl crime saga with a heavy dose of baking—and it means the world to us that you're here for the beginning of it.

What is The Cooling Rack, anyway, you ask? Well, we wanted to have a space to unwind, to share and to discuss everything from the book itself, to our creative processes, to things that have influenced us or continue to influence us on this book. Behind-the-scenes looks at script snippets and corresponding art. Recipes from us and our friends. Letters from you, if you'd be kind enough to send them (and give permission to print them). If it's in any way even remotely related to what *Nutmeg* is about—and isn't the story itself—you can probably find it here. Seeing as this is the first issue, and the first installment of The Cooling Rack, we're just providing a simple introduction to the story as well as a little background on who we are.

You might be wondering just how *Nutmeg* came to be. If we're being completely honest, there isn't really one right answer. The original concept was so far removed from the book you're holding in your hands as to be completely unrecognizable. As you can see, this is not a story about an out-of-work private detective eating expired food items in his pantry to open pathways in his mind and solve cold cases. No, it certainly isn't that. But somewhere in that bizarre premise was the germ of an idea—how there are countless stories of teen detectives, from the classic *Encyclopedia Brown* and the *Hardy Boys* to the more recent *Veronica Mars* and *Flavia de Luce*, but few are the stories told from the perspective of their nemeses. What if there were a book about *Nancy Drew*'s Moriarity? What might that look like?

From there it took on a life of its own as we filtered adolescent antagonism through the tropes of a rise-and-fall crime story. It's as much *Scarface* or *Goodfellas* as it is *Mean Girls*, *Heathers*, and *Heavenly Creatures*. In fact, our elevator pitch has been "*Betty & Veronica* meets *Breaking Bad*."

Of course, it wouldn't be what it is without the art, and Jackie's gentle linework and soft, pastel coloring provides the perfect contrast to the petty criminal elements that will be on display in later issues. And while the narrative hook is teen criminals, we never wallow in

BAKING BAD WITH
Poppy + cassia

by Kevin Johnson

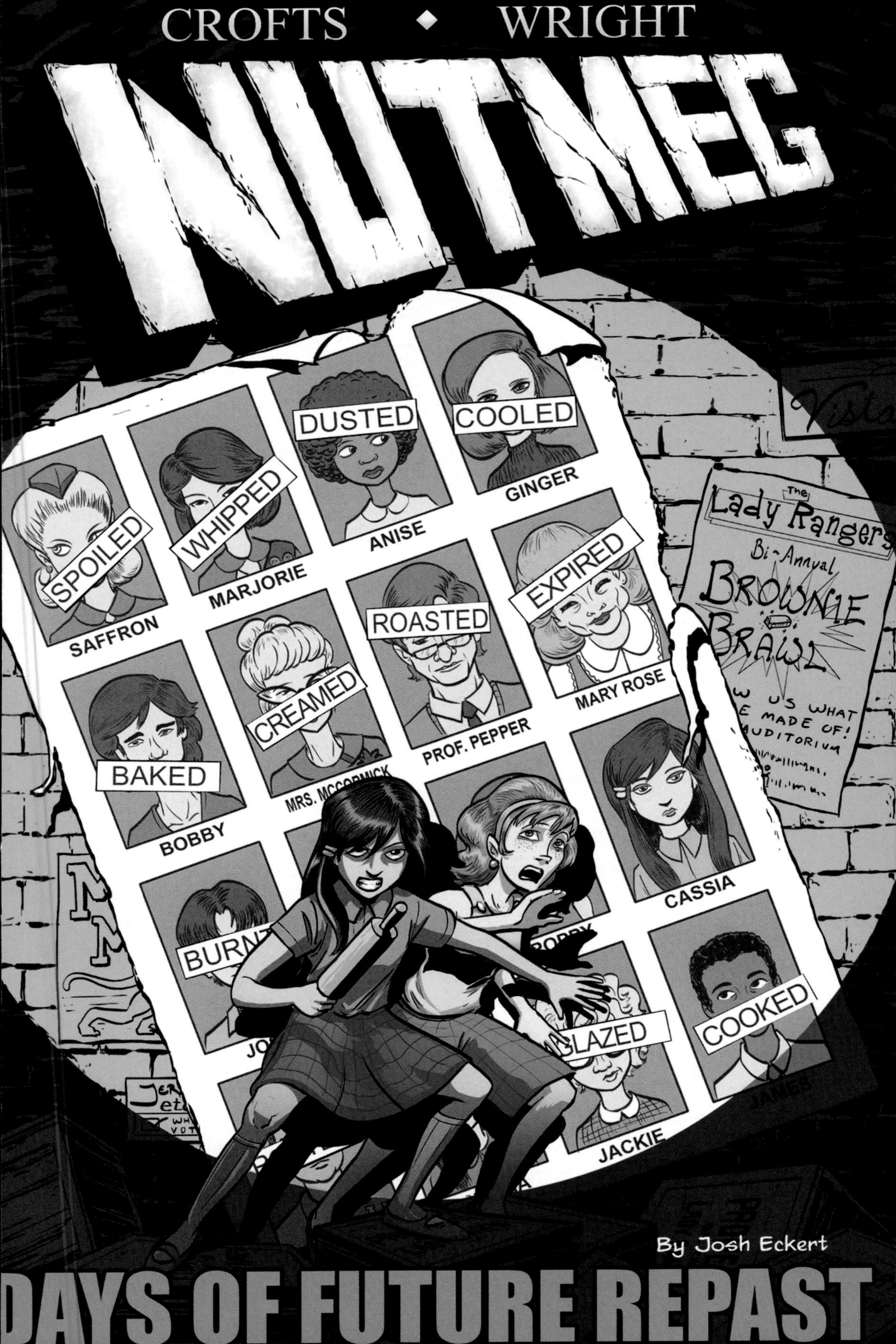
CROFTS • WRIGHT
NUTMEG
DUSTED
COOLED
SPOILED
WHIPPED
GINGER
ANISE
MARJORIE
SAFFRON
EXPIRED
ROASTED
CREAMED
BAKED
MARY ROSE
PROF. PEPPER
MRS. MCCORMICK
BOBBY
CASSIA
GLAZED
COOKED
JACKIE
The Lady Rangers
Bi-Annual
BROWNIE BRAWL
By Josh Eckert
DAYS OF FUTURE REPAST

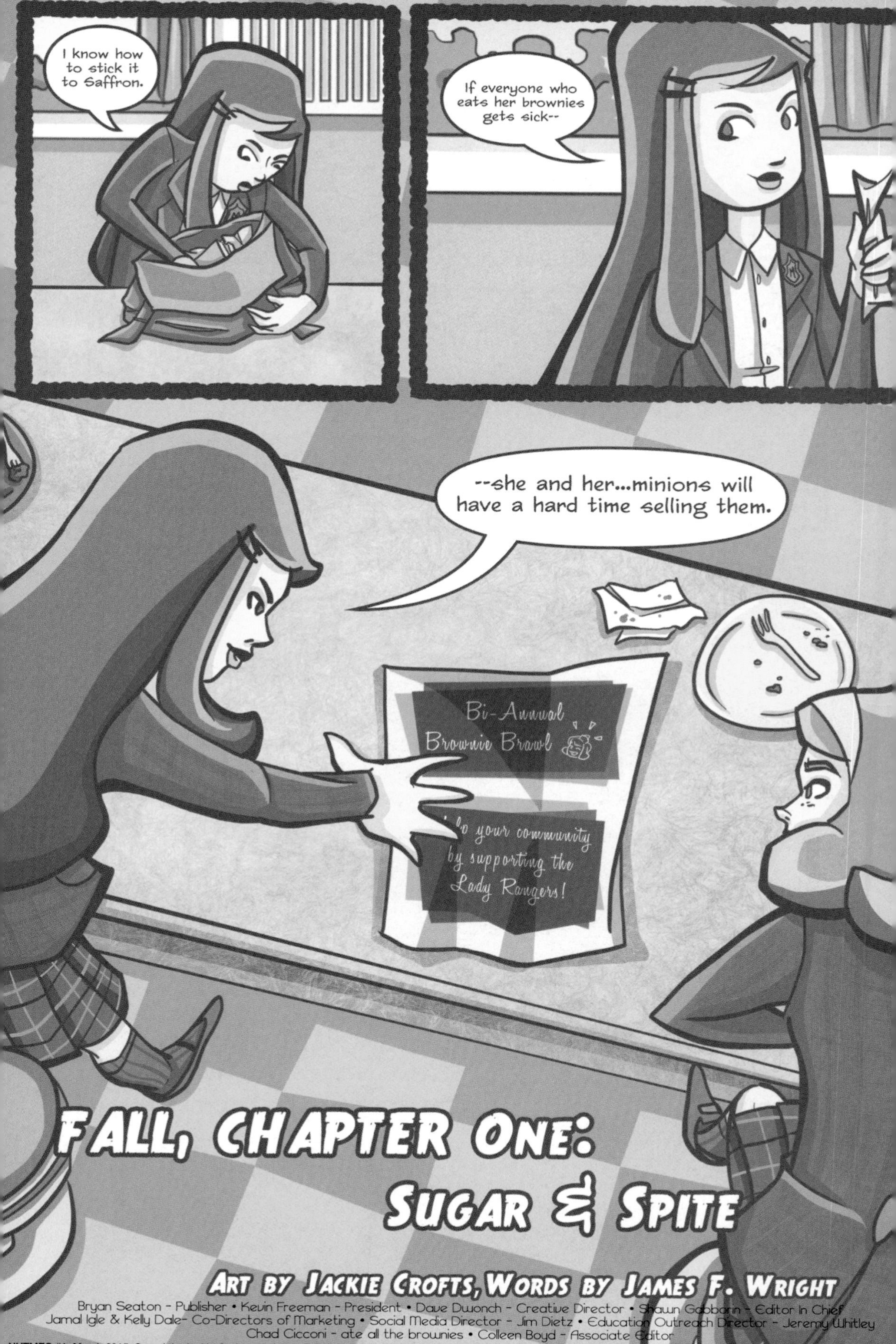
I know how to stick it to Saffron.
If everyone who eats her brownies gets sick--
--she and her...minions will have a hard time selling them.
Bi-Annual Brownie Brawl
by supporting the Lady Rangers!

FALL, CHAPTER ONE: SUGAR & SPITE

ART BY JACKIE CROFTS, WORDS BY JAMES F. WRIGHT

Bryan Seaton - Publisher • Kevin Freeman - President • Dave Dwonch - Creative Director • Shawn Gabborin - Editor In Chief
Jamal Igle & Kelly Dale- Co-Directors of Marketing • Social Media Director - Jim Dietz • Education Outreach Director - Jeremy Whitley
Chad Cicconi - ate all the brownies • Colleen Boyd - Associate Editor

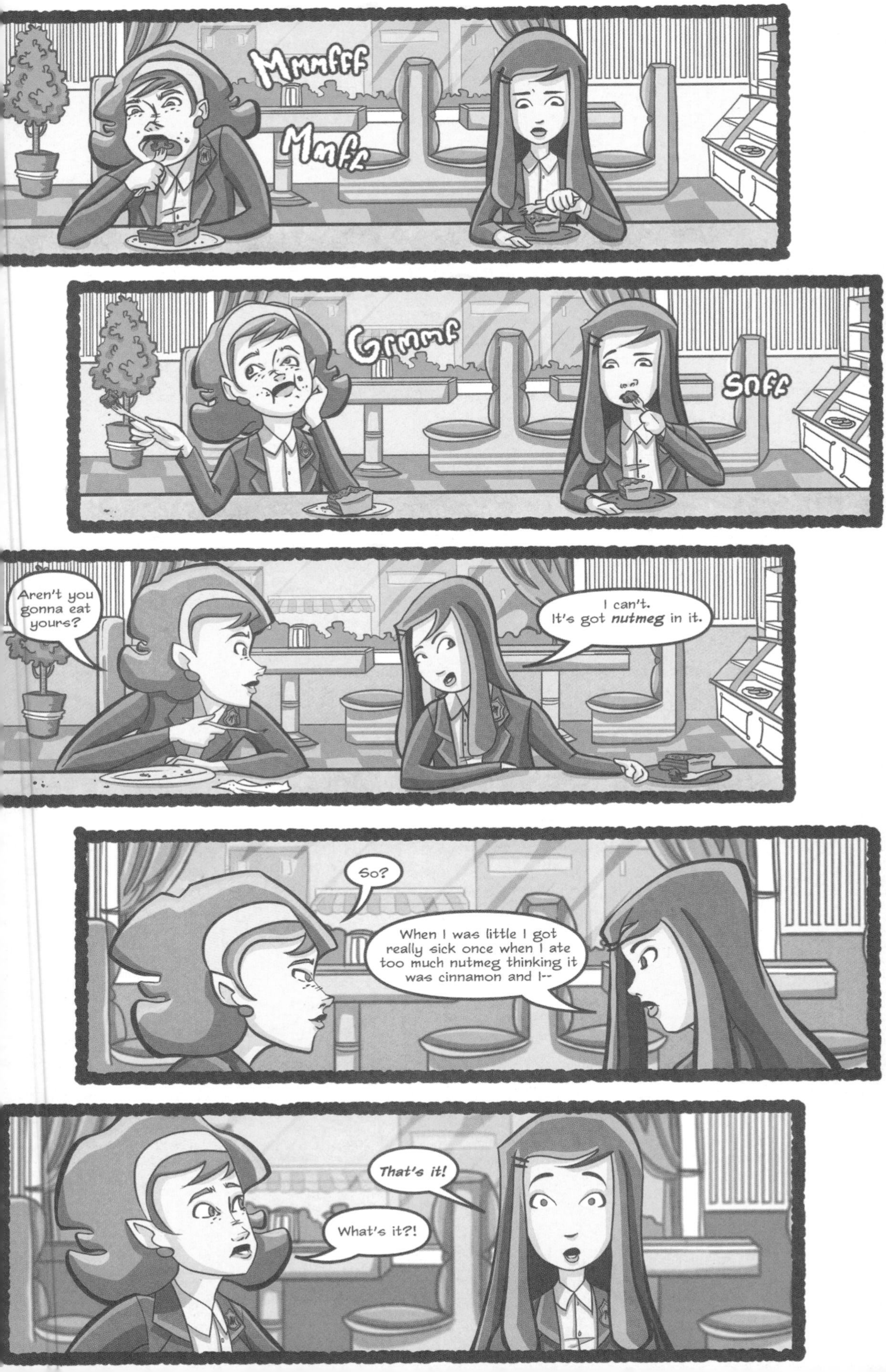
Mmmfff
Mmfff
Grmmf
Snff
Aren't you gonna eat yours?
I can't. It's got *nutmeg* in it.
So?
When I was little I got really sick once when I ate too much nutmeg thinking it was cinnamon and I--
That's it!
What's it?!

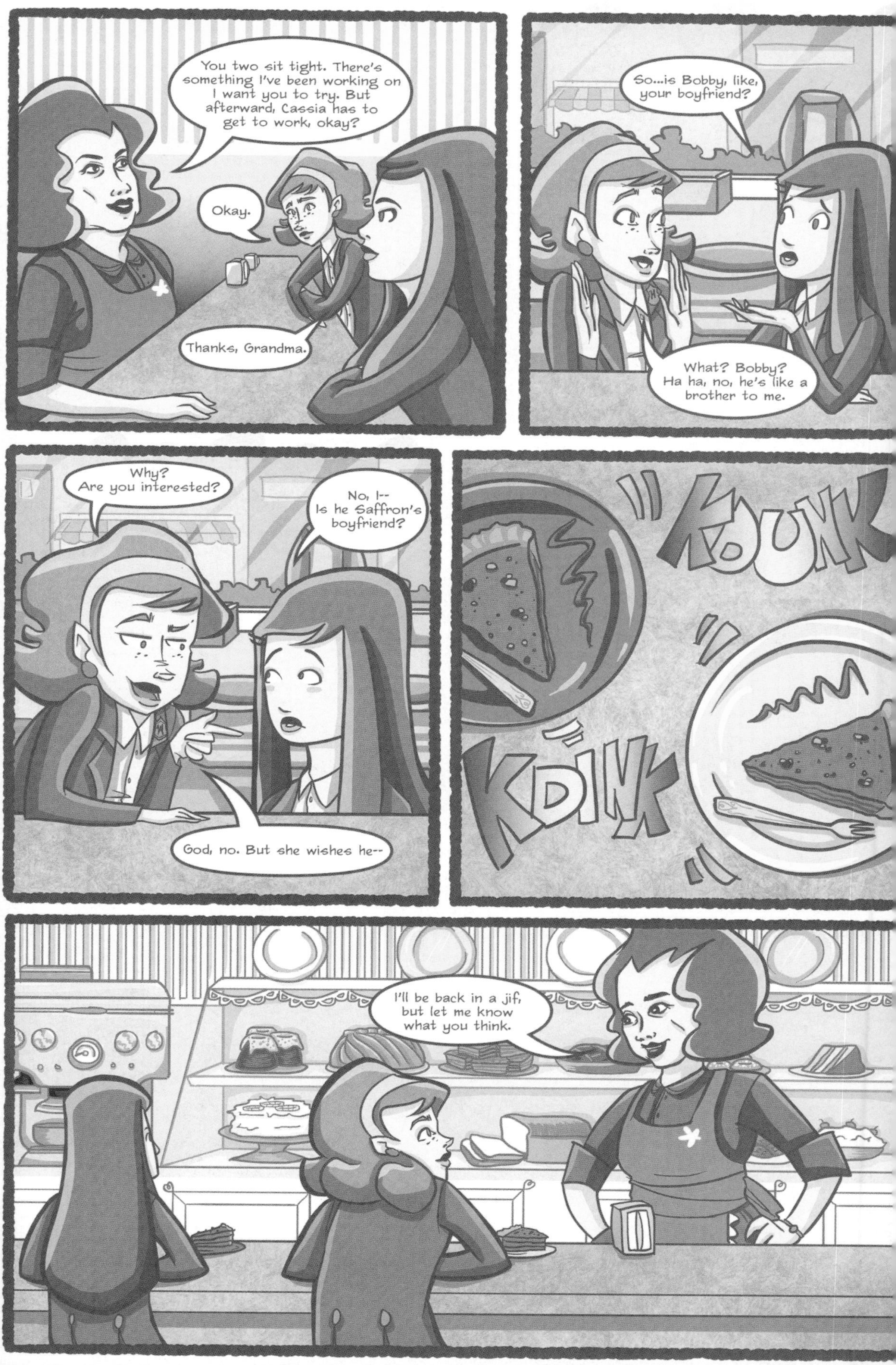
You two sit tight. There's something I've been working on I want you to try. But afterward, Cassia has to get to work, okay?
Okay.
Thanks, Grandma.
So...is Bobby, like, your boyfriend?
What? Bobby? Ha ha, no, he's like a brother to me.
Why? Are you interested?
No, I-- Is he Saffron's boyfriend?
God, no. But she wishes he--
KDUNK
KDINK
I'll be back in a jif, but let me know what you think.

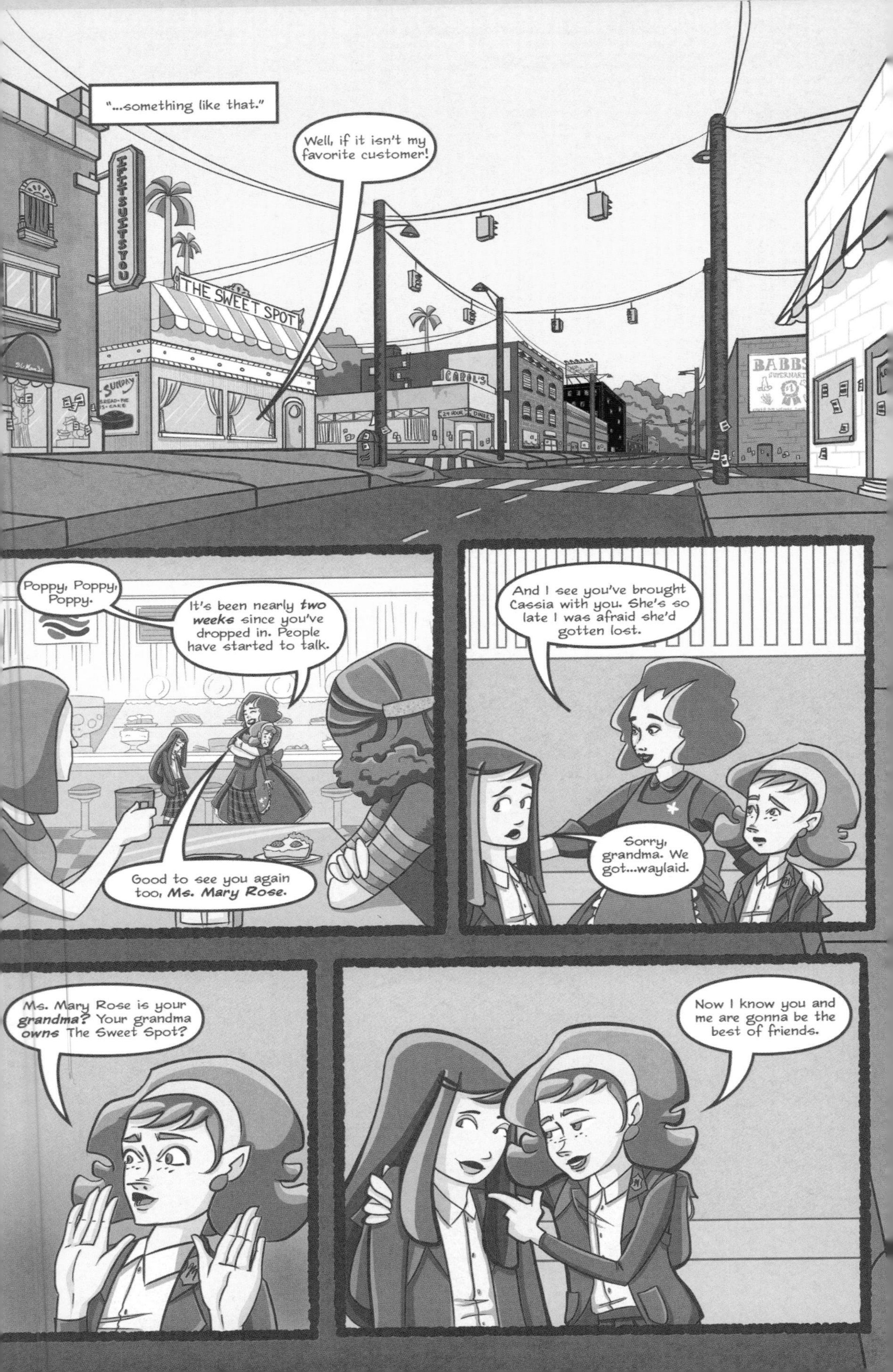

"...something like that."
THE SWEET SPOT
CAROL'S
BABBS
Well, if it isn't my favorite customer!
Poppy, Poppy, Poppy.
It's been nearly **two weeks** since you've dropped in. People have started to talk.
Good to see you again too, **Ms. Mary Rose.**
And I see you've brought Cassia with you. She's so late I was afraid she'd gotten lost.
Sorry, grandma. We got...waylaid.
Ms. Mary Rose is your ***grandma?*** Your grandma ***owns*** The Sweet Spot?
Now I know you and me are gonna be the best of friends.

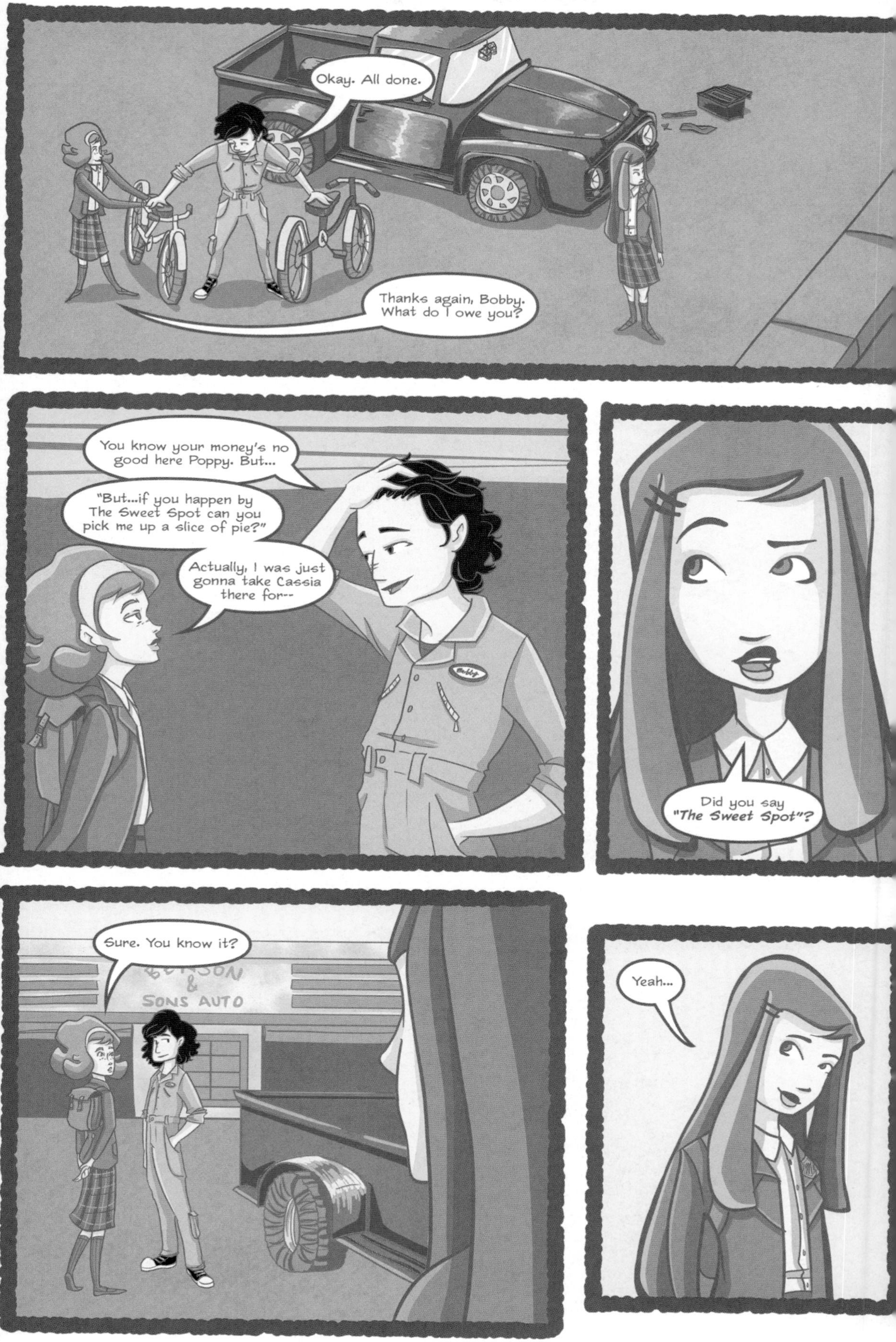
Okay. All done.
Thanks again, Bobby. What do I owe you?
You know your money's no good here Poppy. But...
"But...if you happen by The Sweet Spot can you pick me up a slice of pie?"
Actually, I was just gonna take Cassia there for--
Bobby
Did you say "The Sweet Spot"?
Sure. You know it?
SONS AUTO
Yeah...

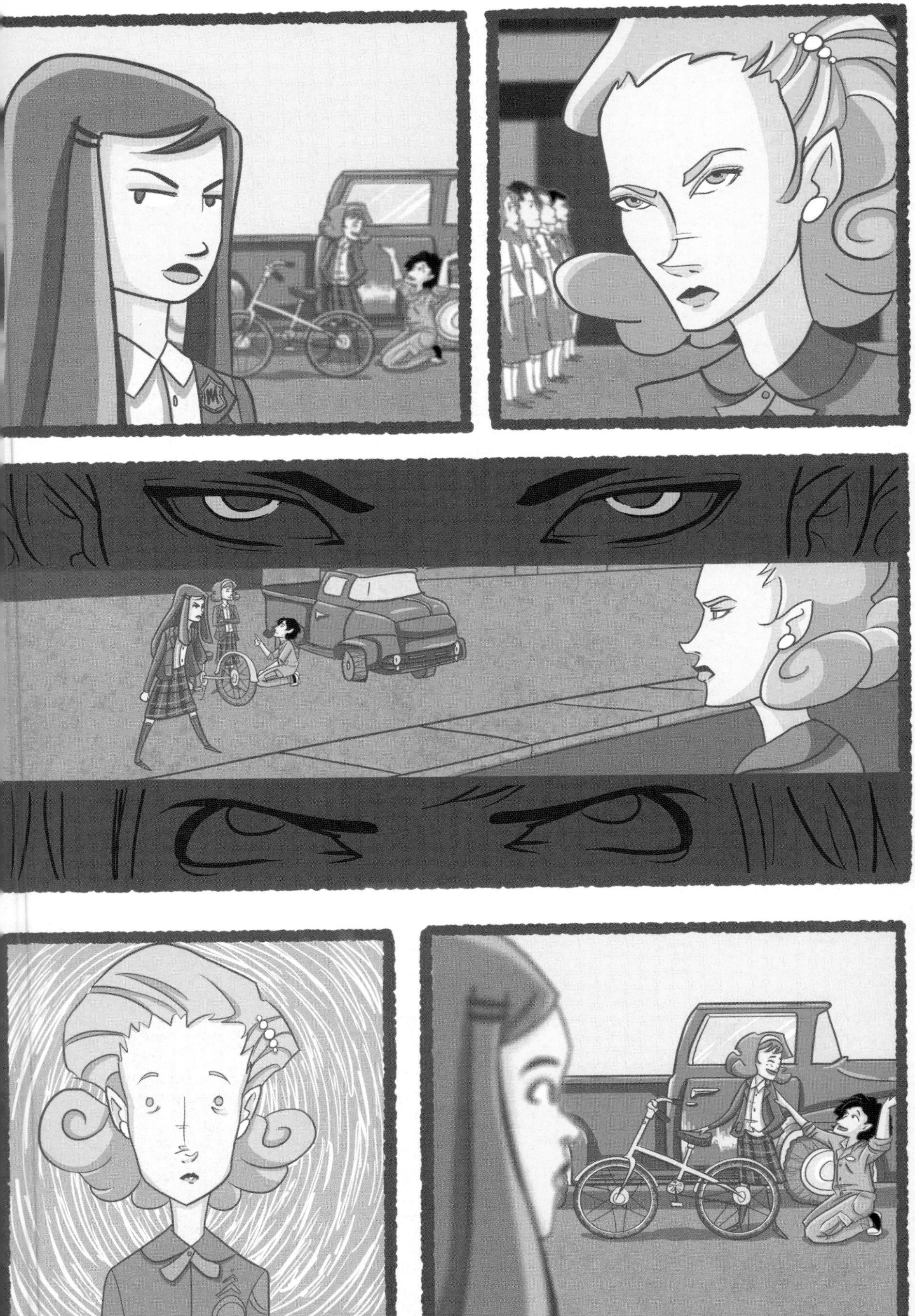

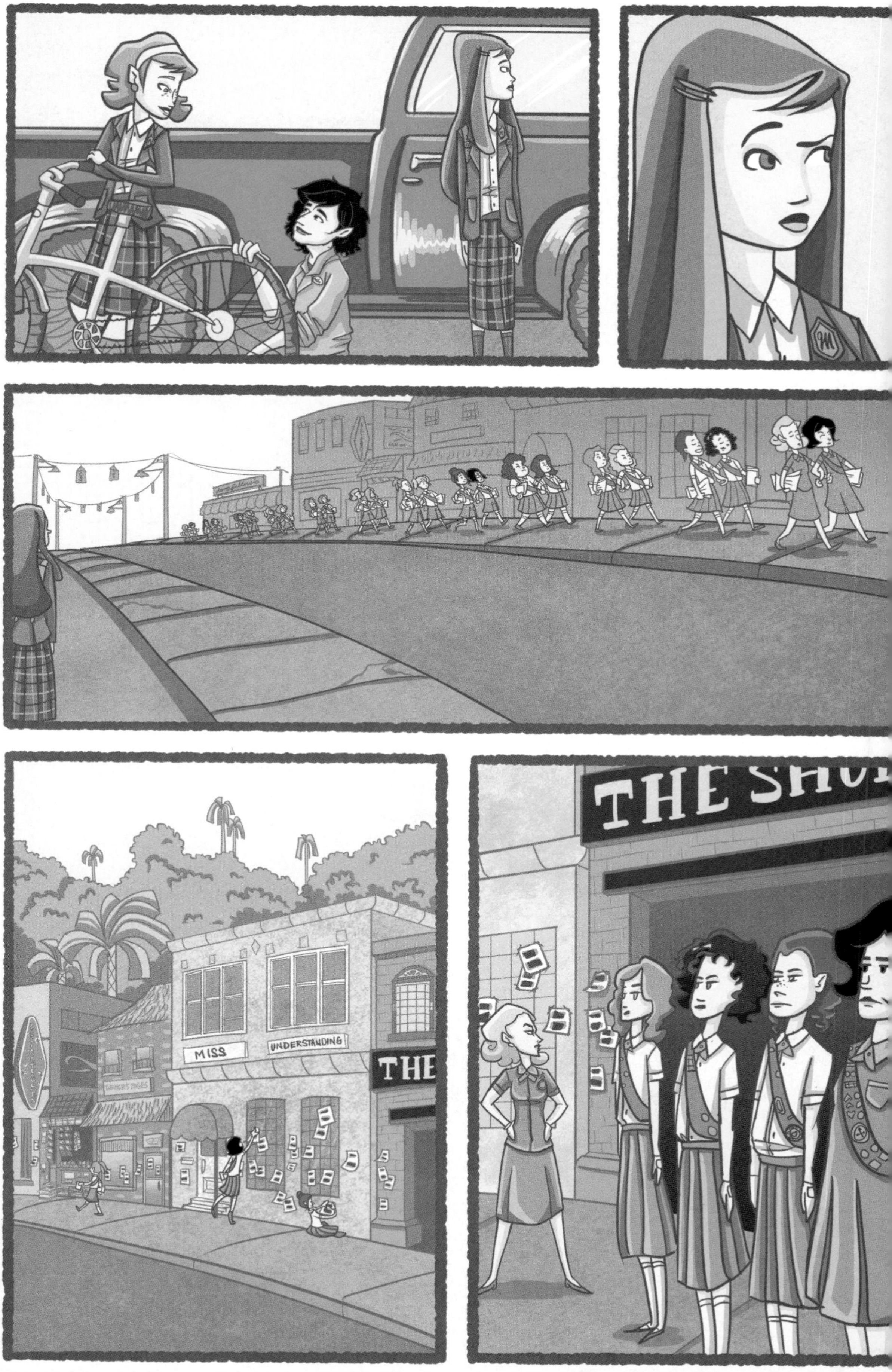
MISS
UNDERSTANDING
THE
THE SH

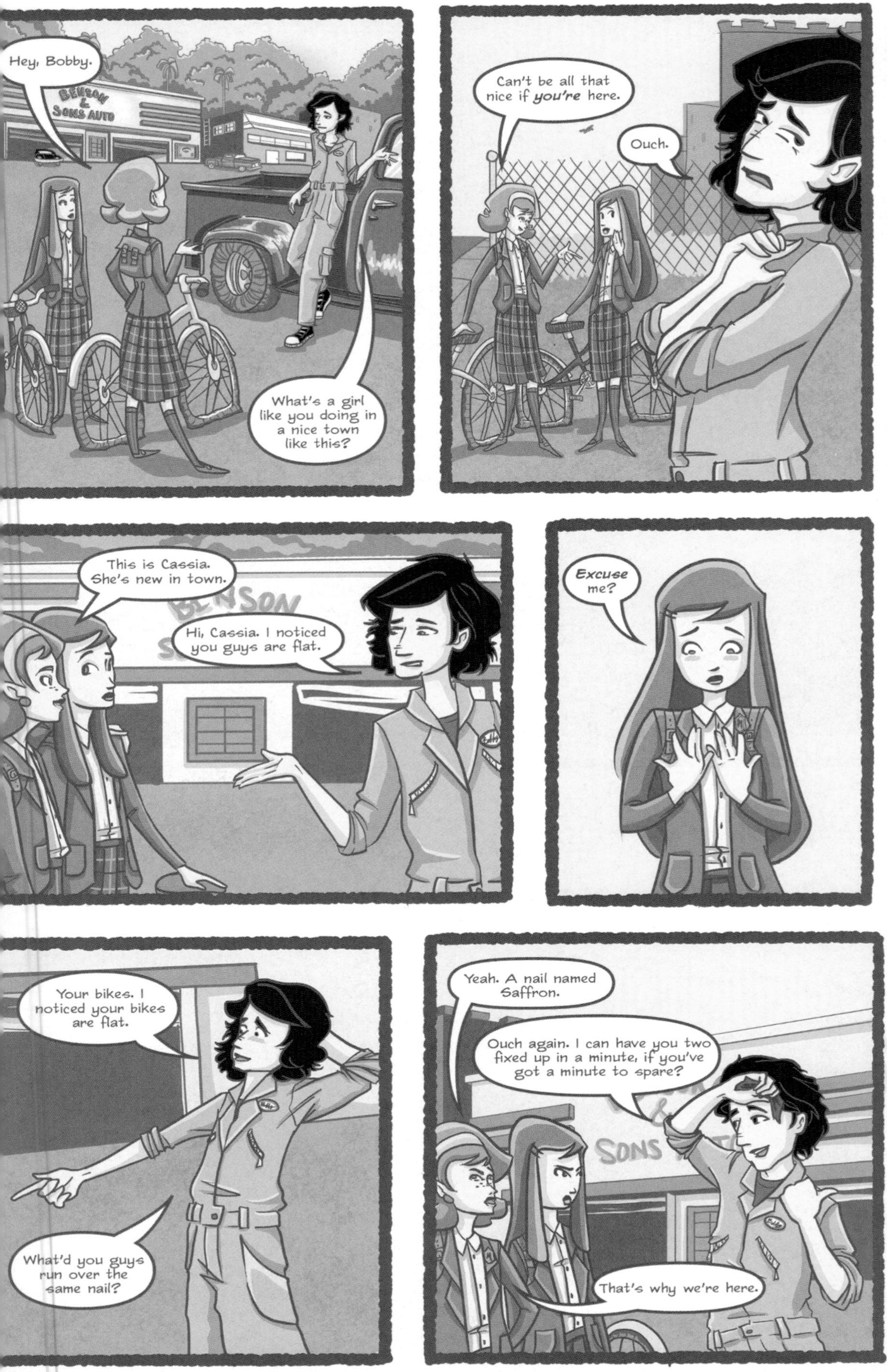
Hey, Bobby.
BENSON & SONS AUTO
What's a girl like you doing in a nice town like this?
Can't be all that nice if *you're* here.
Ouch.
This is Cassia. She's new in town.
Hi, Cassia. I noticed you guys are flat.
Excuse me?
Your bikes. I noticed your bikes are flat.
What'd you guys run over the same nail?
Yeah. A nail named Saffron.
Ouch again. I can have you two fixed up in a minute, if you've got a minute to spare?
That's why we're here.

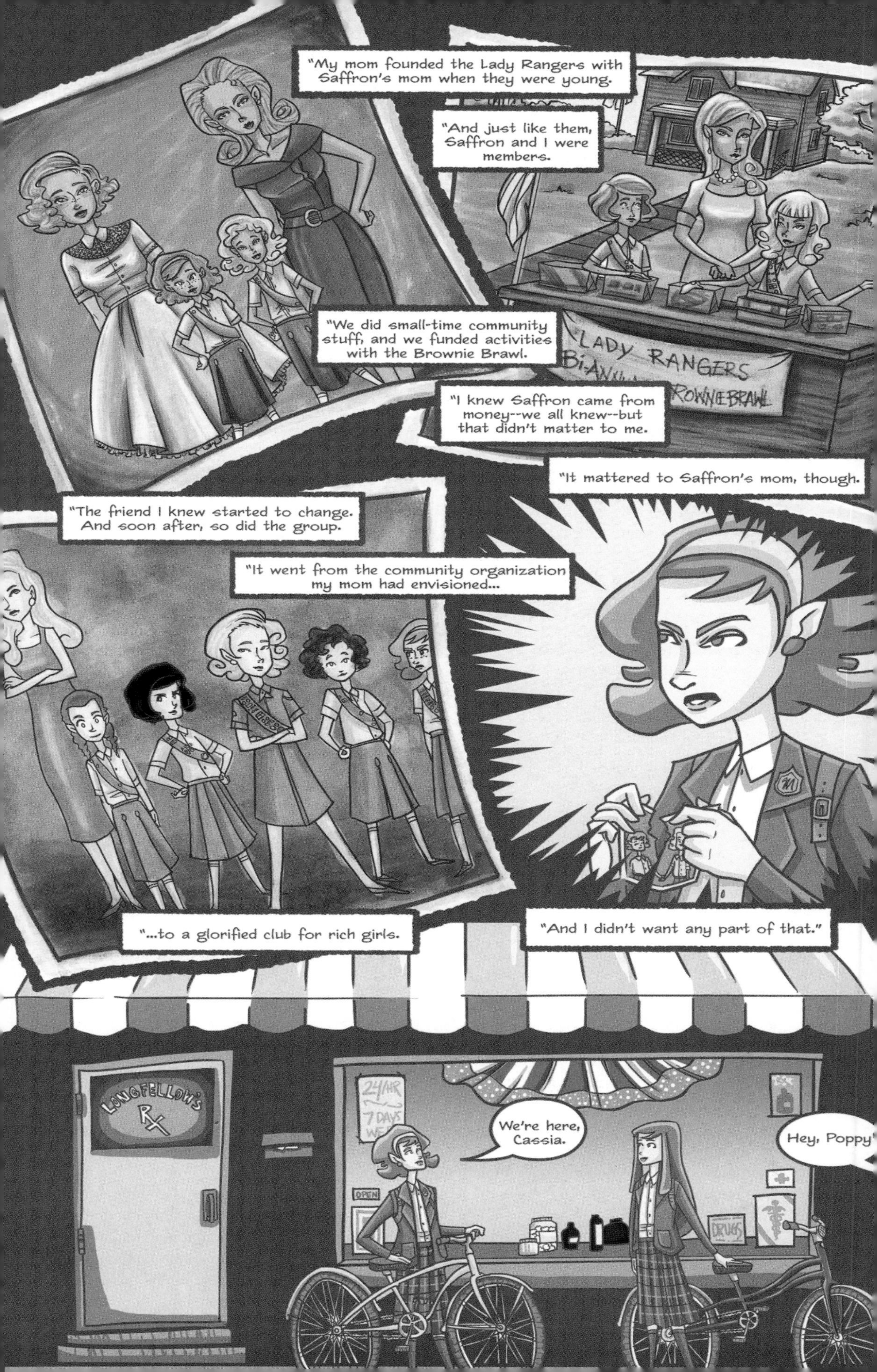
"My mom founded the Lady Rangers with Saffron's mom when they were young.
"And just like them, Saffron and I were members.
"We did small-time community stuff, and we funded activities with the Brownie Brawl.
LADY RANGERS
BROWNIE BRAWL
"I knew Saffron came from money--we all knew--but that didn't matter to me.
"It mattered to Saffron's mom, though.
"The friend I knew started to change. And soon after, so did the group.
"It went from the community organization my mom had envisioned...
"...to a glorified club for rich girls.
"And I didn't want any part of that."
LONGFELLOW'S RX
24/HR
7 DAYS
OPEN
DRUGS
We're here, Cassia.
Hey, Poppy

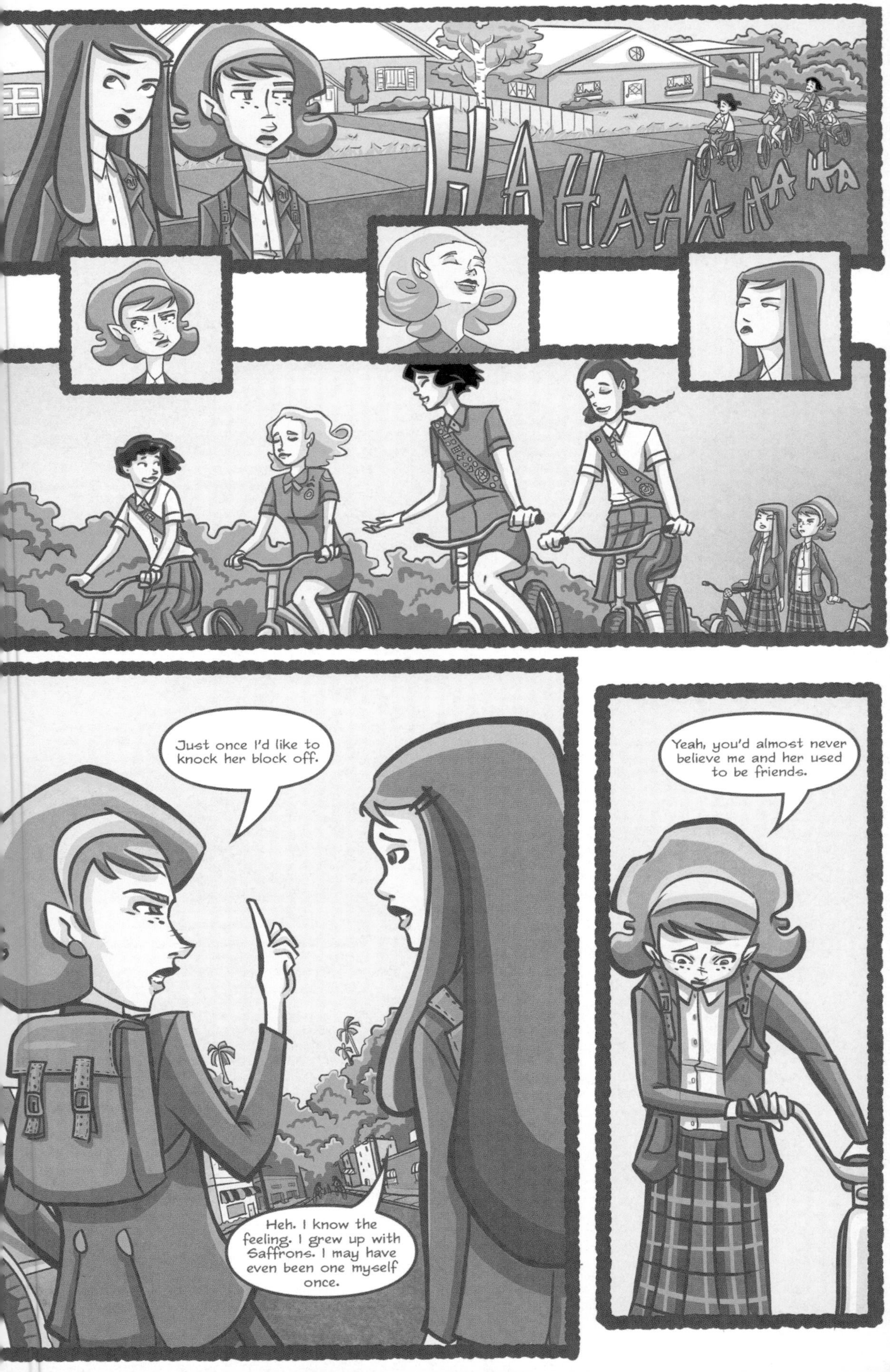
HAHAHAHAHA
Just once I'd like to knock her block off.
Heh. I know the feeling. I grew up with Saffrons. I may have even been one myself once.
Yeah, you'd almost never believe me and her used to be friends.

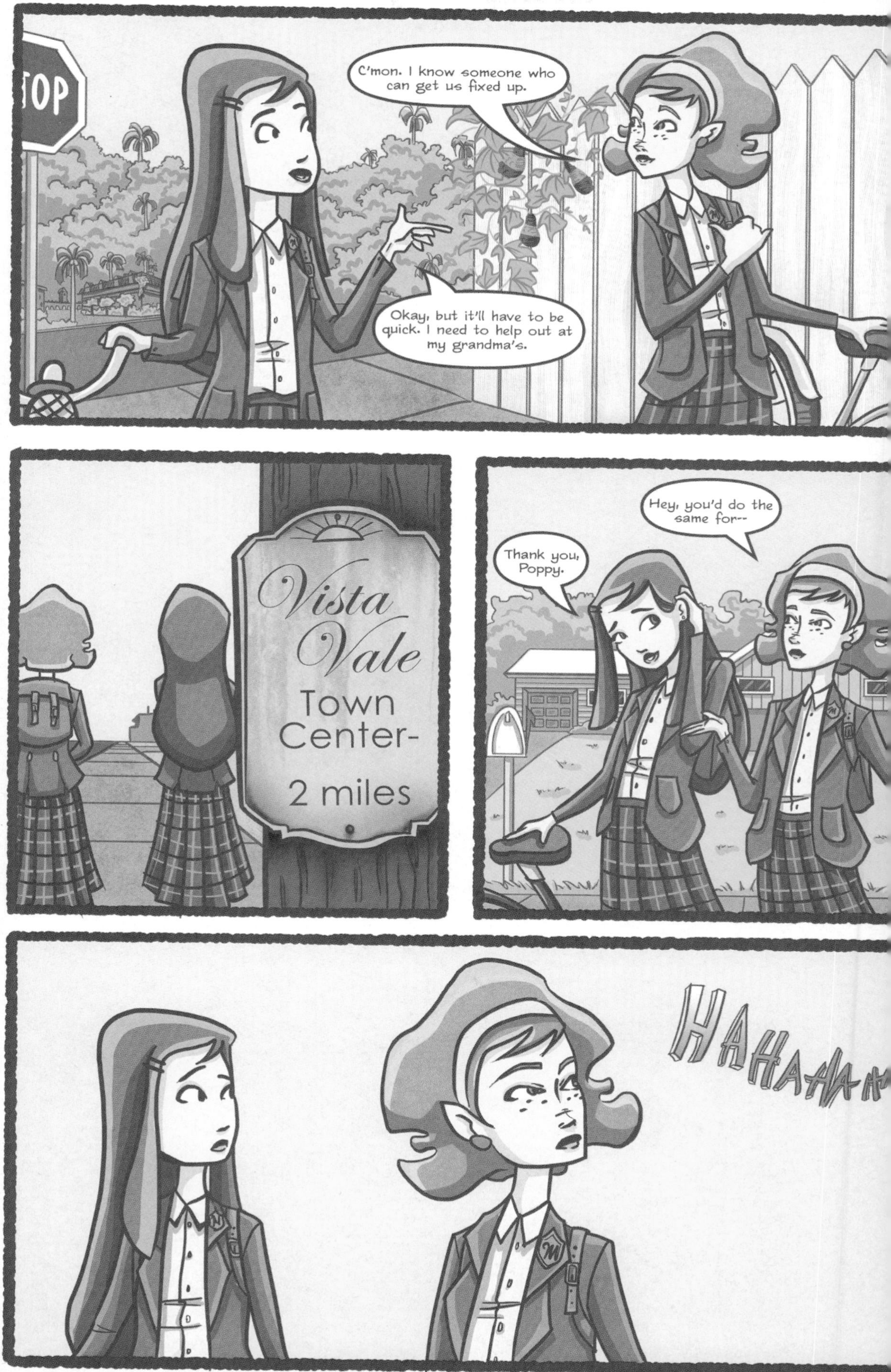

STOP
C'mon. I know someone who can get us fixed up.
Okay, but it'll have to be quick. I need to help out at my grandma's.
Vista Vale Town Center- 2 miles
Hey, you'd do the same for--
Thank you, Poppy.
HAHAHAH

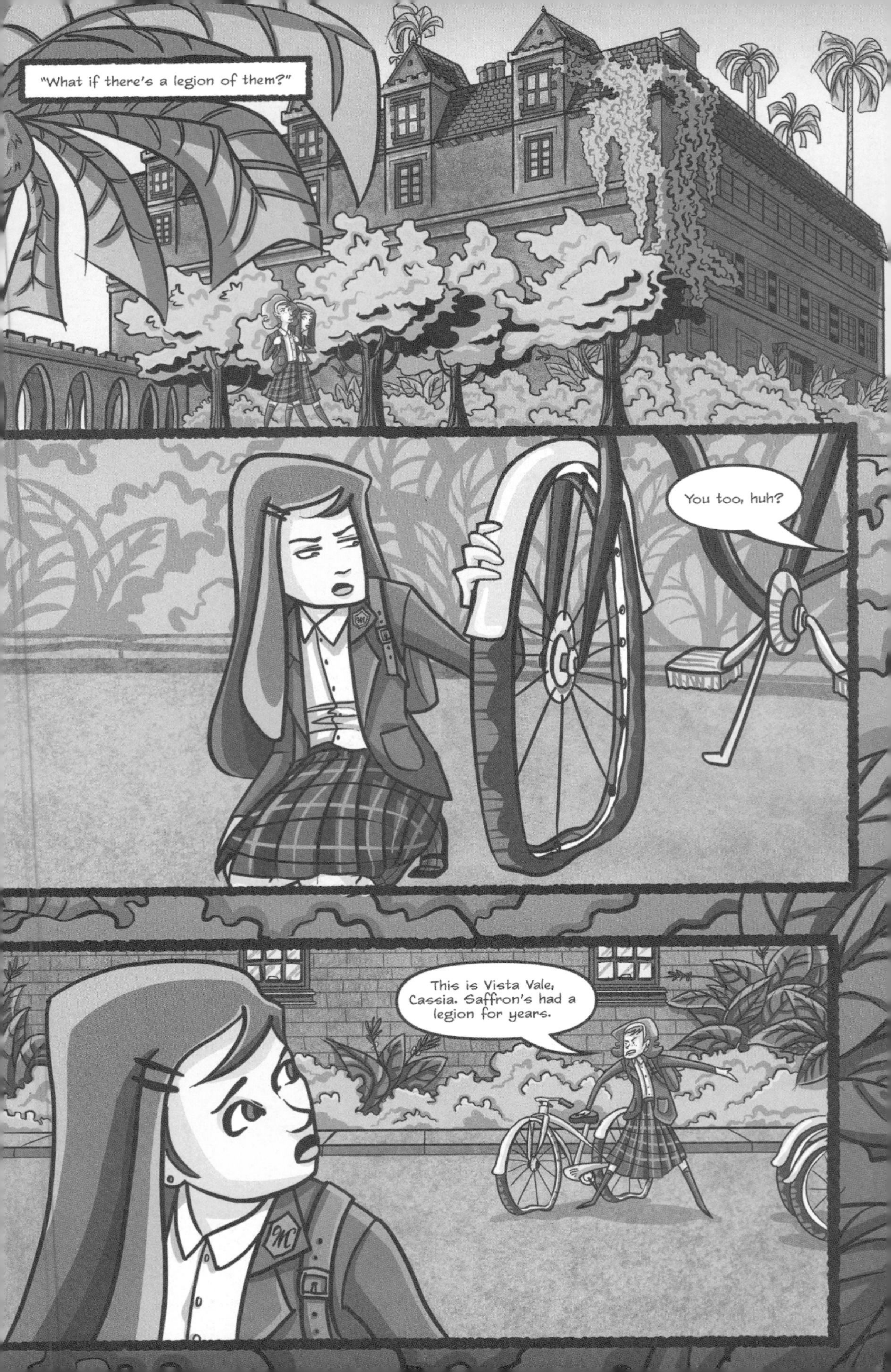
"What if there's a legion of them?"
You too, huh?
This is Vista Vale, Cassia. Saffron's had a legion for years.

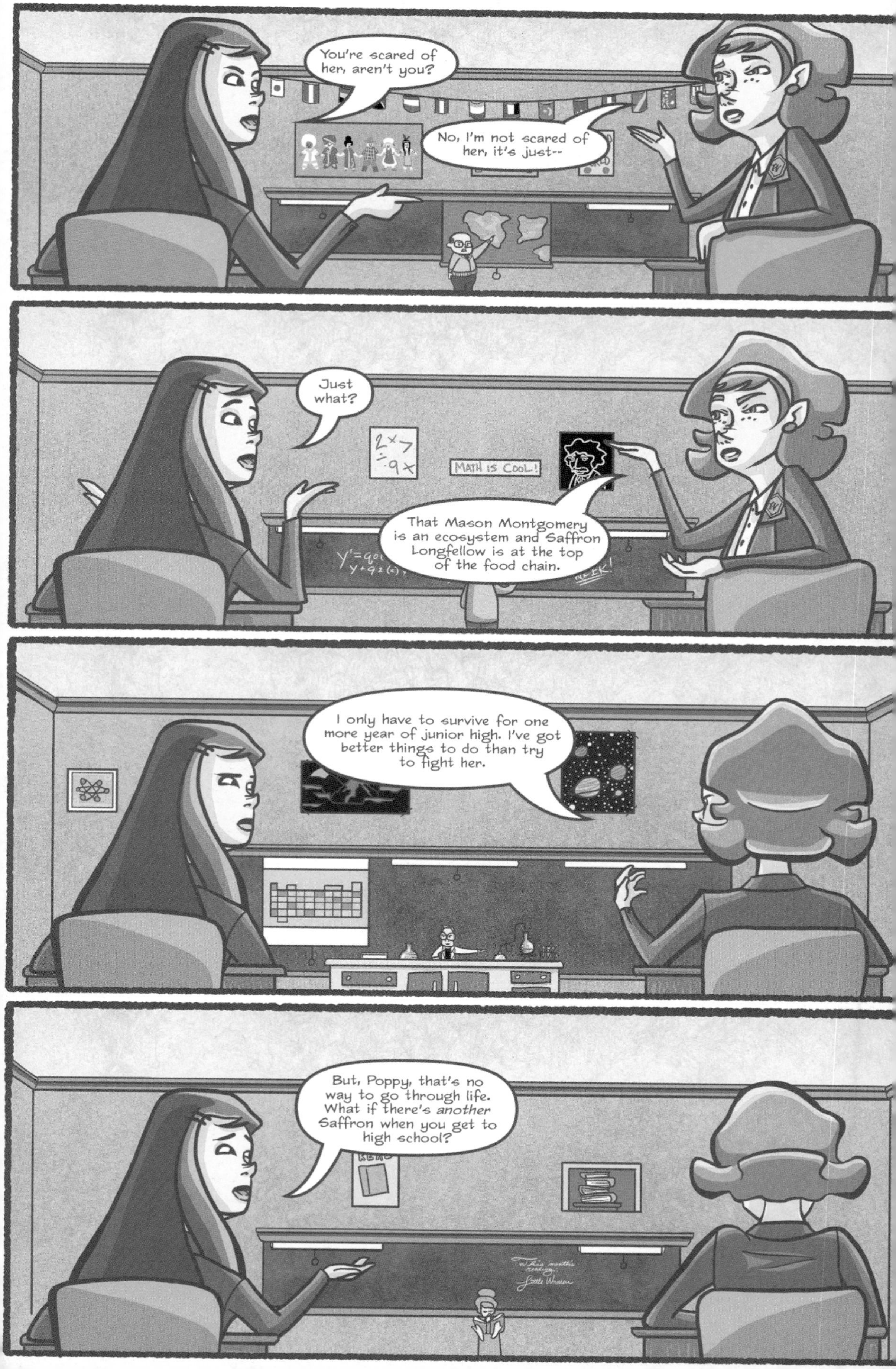

You're scared of her, aren't you?
No, I'm not scared of her, it's just--
Just what?
MATH IS COOL!
That Mason Montgomery is an ecosystem and Saffron Longfellow is at the top of the food chain.
I only have to survive for one more year of junior high. I've got better things to do than try to fight her.
But, Poppy, that's no way to go through life. What if there's *another* Saffron when you get to high school?

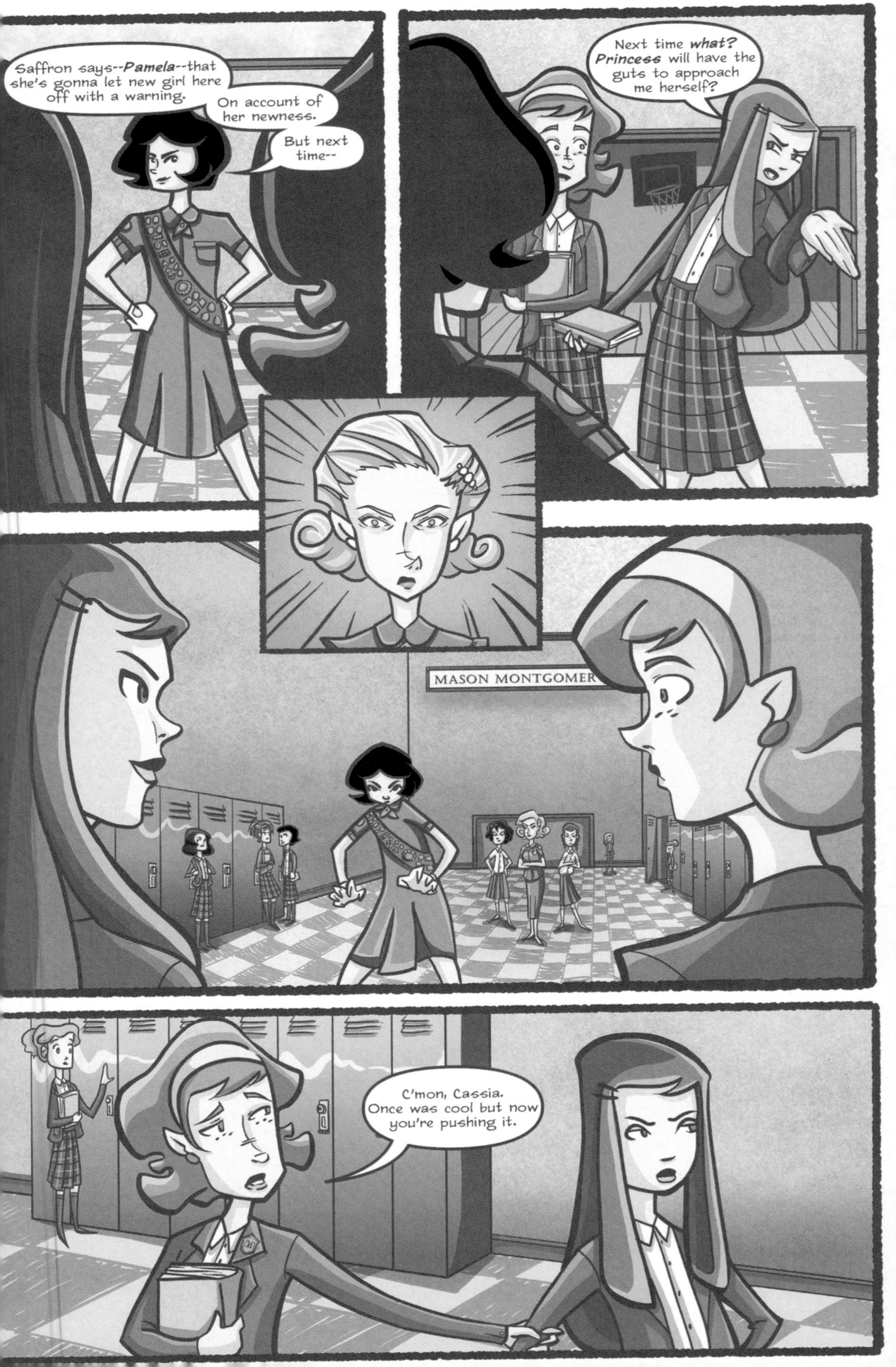
Saffron says--*Pamela*--that she's gonna let new girl here off with a warning.
On account of her newness.
But next time--
Next time ***what? Princess*** will have the guts to approach me herself?
MASON MONTGOMER
C'mon, Cassia. Once was cool but now you're pushing it.

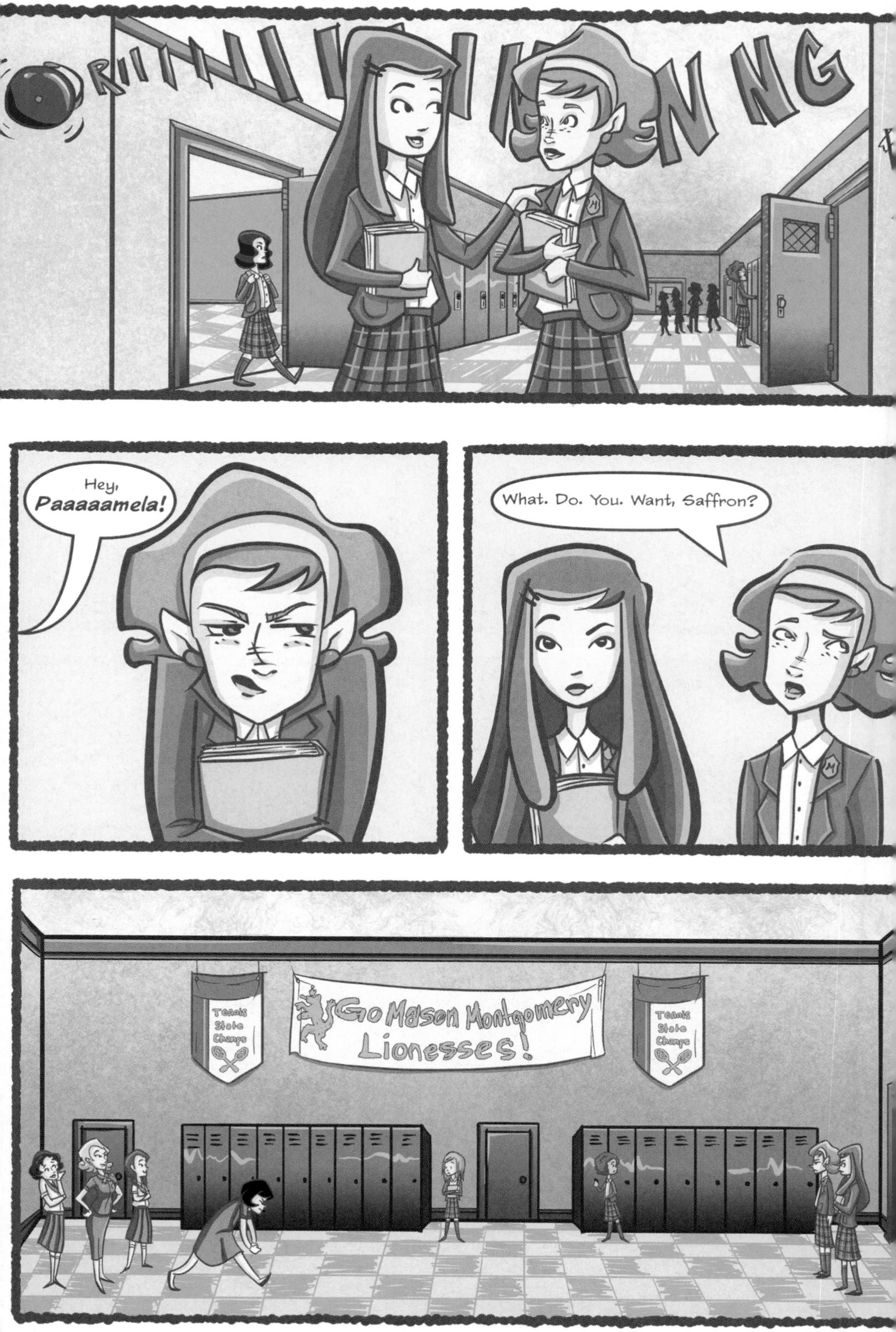

Hey, Paaaaamela!
What. Do. You. Want, Saffron?
Tennis State Champs
Go Mason Montgomery Lionesses!
Tennis State Champs

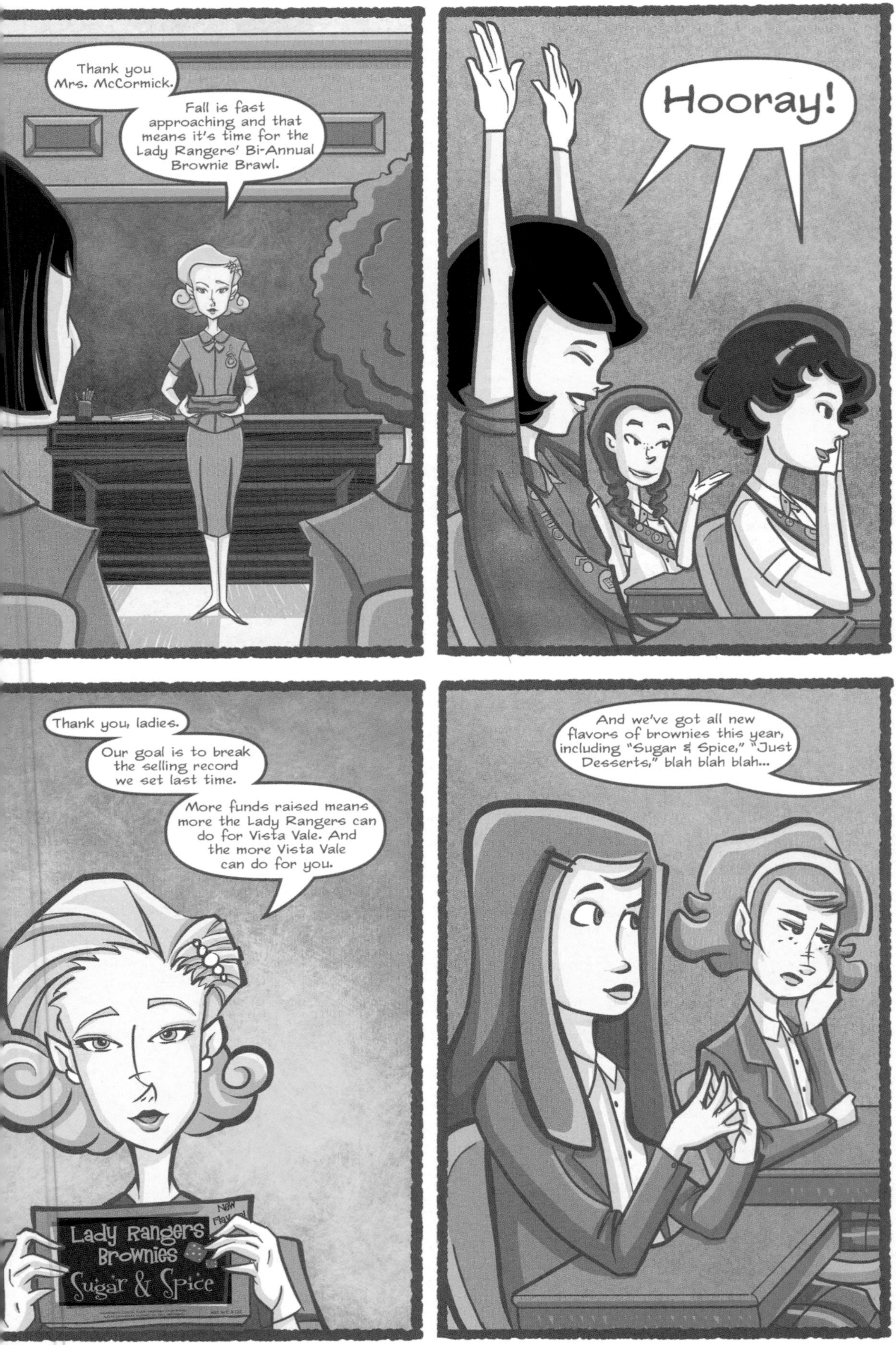
Thank you Mrs. McCormick.
Fall is fast approaching and that means it's time for the Lady Rangers' Bi-Annual Brownie Brawl.
Hooray!
Thank you, ladies.
Our goal is to break the selling record we set last time.
More funds raised means more the Lady Rangers can do for Vista Vale. And the more Vista Vale can do for you.
Lady Rangers Brownies Sugar & Spice
New Flavor!
And we've got all new flavors of brownies this year, including "Sugar & Spice," "Just Desserts," blah blah blah...

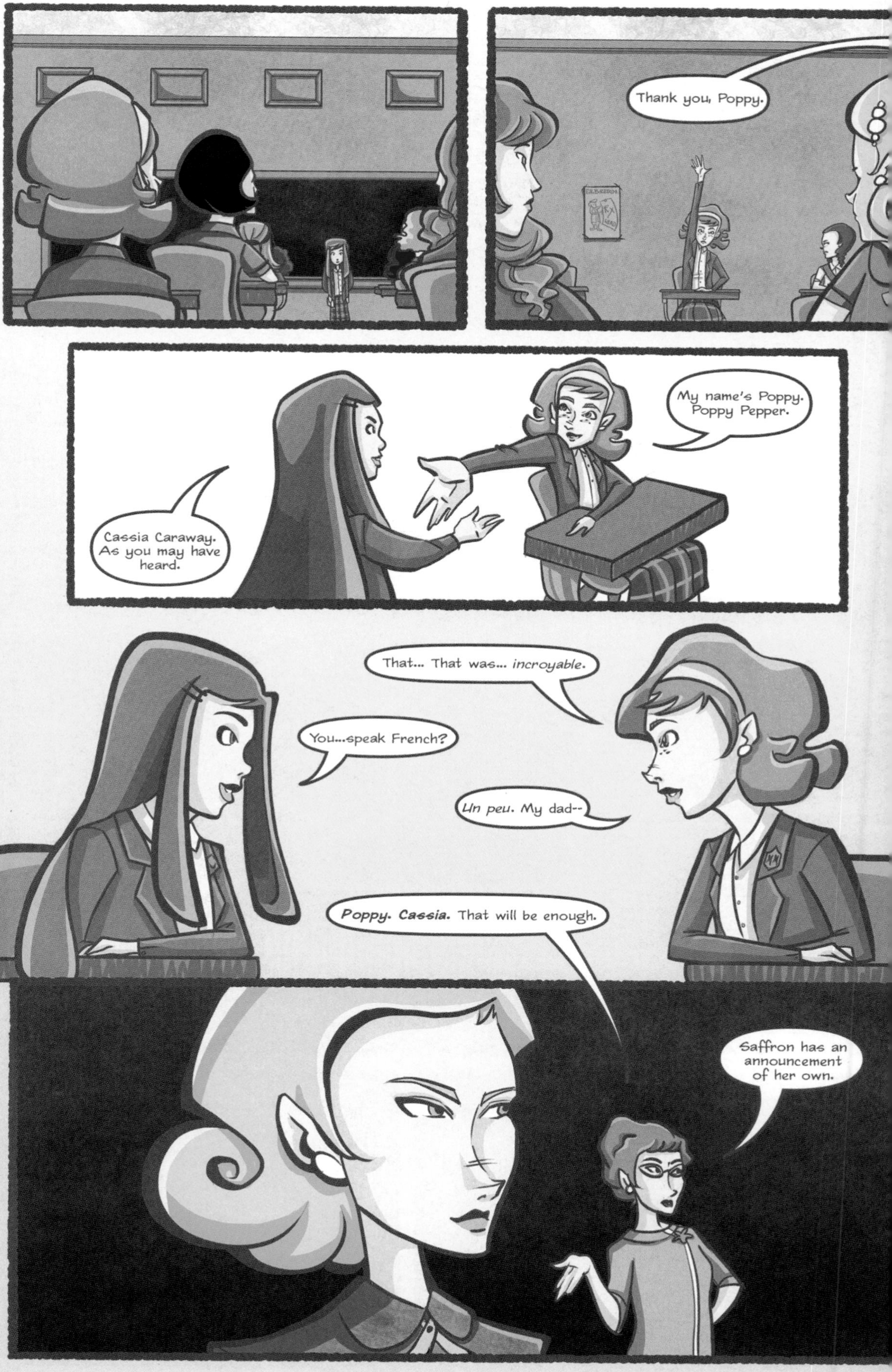
Thank you, Poppy.
My name's Poppy. Poppy Pepper.
Cassia Caraway. As you may have heard.
That... That was... *incroyable*.
You...speak French?
Un peu. My dad--
Poppy. Cassia. That will be enough.
Saffron has an announcement of her own.

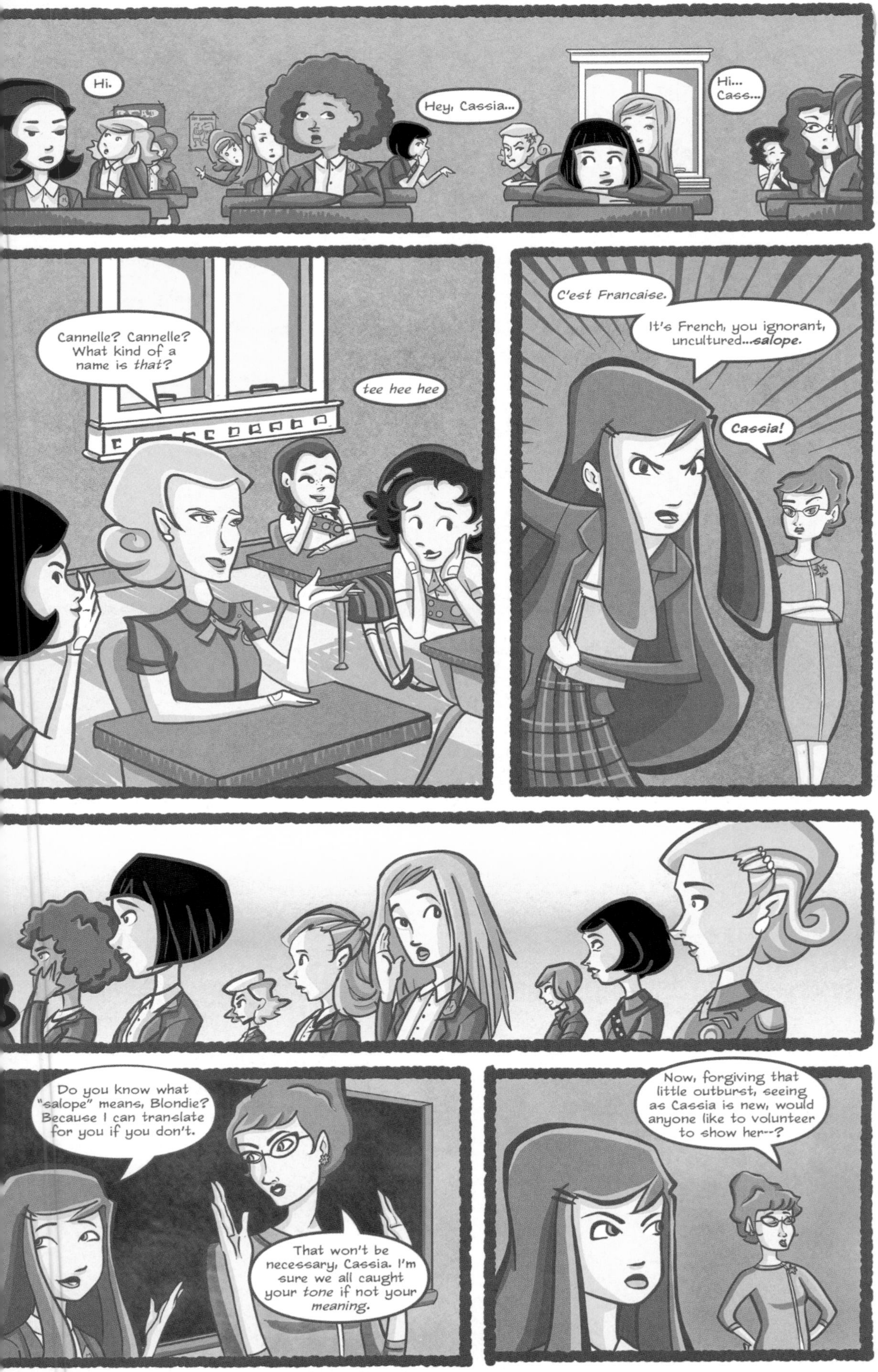
Hi.
Hey, Cassia...
Hi... Cass...
Cannelle? Cannelle? What kind of a name is *that*?
tee hee hee
C'est Francaise.
It's French, you ignorant, uncultured...*salope*.
Cassia!
Do you know what "salope" means, Blondie? Because I can translate for you if you don't.
That won't be necessary, Cassia. I'm sure we all caught your *tone* if not your *meaning*.
Now, forgiving that little outburst, seeing as Cassia is new, would anyone like to volunteer to show her--?